Life's Landscapes

An Anthology

Belle Fourche Writers

Beartown
Press

Contents

Foreword: Battle of the Block by Dale Kringen

Oh, you blank screen of despair! You empty page of defeat! Why must you torment me so? Have I not sacrificed enough time to the gods of creativity to appease you? Night after night I stare into your lonely abyss seeking only the slightest spark of inspiration, and yet you give me nothing in return.

I have no doubt that it would please you greatly if I were to throw my inkwell against the wall and snap my quill into pieces. My impending defeat will certainly bring you inkblots of pleasure. But you shall not defeat me, for the gauntlet has been thrown.

A challenge both made and accepted. We shall meet on the battlefield of prose and fight until victory is mine alone. My mighty quill shall be my sword. Ink shall be my armor. Verbs and nouns are my soldiers. Together we will drive you from the battlefield and back to the darkest recesses of my mind from whence you came.

And as you retreat, broken and beaten, do not expect mercy, as you have shown me none.

"It was late Saturday night, and the ringing of the bells on the front door signaled the final customer of the night."

You see, victory is already mine. . . . I win.

Eric Beeman

Born in the mid 1900's, Eric spent most of his life house painting and doing light construction. Eric served four years in the US Navy, then became an electronics technician. After working 25 years for a government contractor in that occupation, he retired in Belle Fourche, SD.

Leftovers

All the years of living experience gelled down to a savory dish
Artwork, writing, music, construction, decorating, education
Cooking, brewing, bubbling into something unique
Perhaps, if lucky, something many will enjoy
Not always to everyone's taste
Had to find the right mix
To blend with the hard lessons
Peaceable, salted with a relaxed spirit
Fold in older, broken, more patient, tolerant ingredients
Hoping for more, settling for less, stronger, weaker
A satisfying stew simmering through all the storms of life

We Still Have Three Kids

Just after Reagan was elected president, I moved my wife and three kids out west to the mountains. Why I did so is another story.

We sold our house in Minnesota, and I took five thousand dollars and stuffed it into my front pocket. I had an old, rusty green 1952 Ford one ton pickup and a thirteen-foot long Aljo camping trailer given to me by a friend.

When I hooked up the trailer, I noticed that the overload spring shackles were broken, so on our way, I stopped at another friend's place, and he helped me locate a similar pair. We replaced them the same day.

Finally on our way, we began the journey west across South Dakota. First, we stopped in Aberdeen for a night, then headed up to Highway Two in North Dakota.

We must have stopped somewhere in North Dakota, but I don't remember where. I do remember that the landscape was flat and barren. Our next stop was Havre, Montana. It was like driving down into an oasis.

It's a good thing we didn't spend much time sightseeing. There weren't any sights up there on the Hi-Line. Finally, we came to the foothills of the

Rocky Mountains. There was a KOA campground near Libby, Montana that we camped at for a night. It was such a refreshing break from the high desert we'd just crossed.

We got back on the road with a renewed interest in the adventure. After a few miles, I wanted to pull over and let the traffic by. My 1952 Ford pulling a trailer seemed to always have traffic behind it. A pullover did come up, and we veered off the road to the right. There was just enough room for the truck and trailer. Trees came nearly up to the road. This pullover was at the bottom of a hill. When we got back on the road, we would have to climb another hill.

My wife, my two-year-old son, and I got out of the truck. Then I went around the back and helped my four and five-year-old daughters out.

There was a well-established path that led down into the trees. We all walked down through the trees, and then we happened upon train tracks. I was standing on one side of the tracks, and my wife was on the other. I don't remember which side the kids were on. All of a sudden, I heard something and looked up to see a freight train bearing down on us. All I could do was yell, "Get off the tracks!" Then the loud train rushed by at maybe seventy miles per hour, and in a few seconds, it was gone. A deafening roar of death on wheels.

Then silence.

I looked around anxiously. My wife was there. The three kids were there. It was okay. Nobody was hurt.

I still have flashbacks of the incident. Sometimes I wonder if I didn't lose someone and that somehow, it's been blotted out of my memory.

No. We only have three kids. Thank God Almighty. They're still all okay.

Coming of Age

Spearfish, South Dakota

December 20,1990

"Last call for Red Bird 24 to Sioux Falls," Driver Sylvester (Sly) Milner yelled as he threw the last of the baggage into storage. As he was pulling the door down, a lady ran out of the terminal screaming, "Wait, Wait!"

Sly begrudgingly lifted the baggage door back up. "Lady, one second later and you'd be SOL."

"Thank you, sweetie pie. Your ride would be really boring without me, now wouldn't it. You know it would." She handed him her bag and boarded the bus. Kristie Kettleson was heading for Chicago where she grew up. Her parents were well to do and gave her everything she needed for a good life. She didn't listen to or take advantage of the opportunities offered and instead spent her time trying to impress those around her with whomever she could hang on her arm. Now middle-aged, she was going back home for a break. Her ex-husband had the kids for the two-week Christmas break, and that would give her time to relax and unwind. As she made her way down the aisle of the bus, she was relieved to see that half the seats were empty. She spied a seat near a couple of younger guys that she might have interesting conversation with. She smiled at them, said hi, and sat down.

Sly made a quick inspection around the bus. He was keeping an eye on the first set of dual wheels. The inside tire on the left side was wearing more than the rest. Everything else looked okay, so he made his way around to get on board. As he was getting in, another driver standing by the terminal warned him about a storm heading in from the west. "They say we could get dumped on."

Sly nodded. "We should be long gone before then." He boarded, picked up the intercom mic, and announced, "Okay, everybody, we're leaving right on time." He sat down and made himself comfortable. After taking the air brake off, he put the Allison automatic in drive, and the big machine began moving forward. He liked the feel of a 350 horse Cummins diesel taking him wherever he wanted. Spearfish was a nice little town and reminded him of Bozeman, Montana. After he was at cruising speed and starting what was arguably the most boring route in the country, he sat back and made himself relax.

Suddenly, he heard an outburst of hysterical laughter from the back. Kristie was getting along well with one of the male passengers. His name was Jim Hanby. Jim was on his way to Blue Earth, Minnesota, to see his mother for Christmas. Presently, he was living with his wife in Bonners Ferry, Idaho. Tall, well built, and friendly made him the perfect guy that Kristie could have fun conversation with. Sly was hoping he wouldn't have to listen to her cackle all the way to Sioux Falls. That was the end of his route, and he would then head back in the other direction.

The bus made a stop in Rapid City and picked up another 19 passengers. That made it a little uncomfortable for Kristie, plus Jim was starting to talk about life in north Idaho, and after saying, "That's nice," she turned around in her seat and was quiet.

The next stop was Wall. There would be an exchange of passengers and fuel would be added. Three passengers got off, and four boarded. Sly noticed the eyes of a young girl about 12. One was blue and the other brown. The odd thing was that it gave him an uneasy feeling. Also, before she sat down, she scanned the bus looking at everybody. They all looked at her, then looked away. Her name was Lisa.

As the bus left the on ramp and continued down the interstate, Lisa stood up and said loud enough for Sly to hear, "We should go back."

Sly didn't respond right away because of the strangeness of it, but then he finally said, "Sorry, girl, but we have to keep going. Are you going to be alright?"

"Yes," she said in a polite, quiet voice. "I'll be fine."

The Detour

The bus had only gone about 25 miles when they came to a detour to the north. A tractor trailer had turned over and blocked both eastbound lanes. There were highway patrol cars, a fire truck, and a tow truck on the scene, and it looked like they had it mostly cleaned up. The bus was the last in a line of about 10 vehicles, and as they headed up toward Philip, the detour signs were taken down and traffic resumed on the interstate. This was going to cause quite a delay, so Sly called it in that they were going to be late getting to their next stop.

It was around 4:30 pm when they made a right turn toward Philip. The cars were getting further ahead, but Sly didn't care. He kept his speed at sixty-five. After another 12 miles, he saw the caution sign directing them to slow down to 10 miles per hour.

Boy, he thought, *what's going on here?* And before he had a chance to react, the bus lurched to the right and into a shallow ditch. There was a lone old oak tree with a large branch that cracked the windshield and scraped across the top of the bus. They came to a stop in soil that was soft and somewhat muddy. Sly set the brake and stood up. "Is everybody okay?" He waited and looked around.   No one was hurt, and the bus was intact and upright. "I'm going to try and drive up onto the road. Don't worry. I'm not going to get crazy." He took the brake off and tried to move the bus. There were a few inches of movement, but he knew it was hopeless. He decided to radio in.

"Red Bird 24 to base, come in," he said and waited. Nothing. "Red Bird 24 to base, come in, please." Still nothing.

Sly stood up again. "People, may I have your attention. We're stuck and the radio is out. I know you've got lots of good questions right now, but I don't have any answers. I'm going to see if I can get the radio going. Be assured someone is going to find us here before too long. But we do have a full tank of fuel, so we will be comfortable even if we have to wait till morning."

"Morning!" said Kristie. "I need to get to Chicago."

Sly didn't respond. He put on his jacket and made his way outside. He walked up onto the road so he could get a better look at the roof of the bus. "Yes," he said, noticing the missing antenna.

It was getting dark, and the storm was moving in. As he stood there, he wondered what had happened to the traffic. Nothing in both directions. Then he remembered that crews had almost cleaned up the mess on the interstate when they took the detour. He should have just waited.

Out into the Storm

Jim Hanby got out of his seat and started making his way to the door. "Where are you going, sweetie?" Kristie said with a toothy smile.

Jim looked back. "I'm just going to stretch my legs."

She sat there for a minute, anxious, then got up and started for the door herself.

Lisa stood up and said to her, "Don't go out there."

Kristie hissed back, "Mind your own business, you little freak."

As she was getting off the bus, the wind was picking up, and snow was starting to fall. She saw Sly standing on the road, but Jim was a little way further up in the ditch. "Hey, come here and look at this!" yelled Jim.

Both Kristie and Sly walked over to him. "What have you got there?" Sly said as he approached.

Jim just stood looking down. Sly and Kristie gathered around and noticed a funny smell. Jim looked up angrily but said nothing. Kristie had seen that look before and instantly put her hand in her purse and grabbed the handle of her 38-caliber pistol. She felt strong and almost invincible.

Sly also saw the look on Jim's face and instinctively raised his hands halfway up in self-defense. He also noticed the odor. He thought to himself, "What are these two thinking? I'm going to have to do something."

Jim had seen the two approaching, and by that time, his thoughts were racing. *Why did they come over here? What are they going to do? These guys better back off and now.*

Kristie was thinking, *I'll shoot Jim first, then the driver.*

Sly was thinking, *It's time. If I backhand the girl first, I might be able to take down this guy, but I'd better be fast.*

Jim thought, *I really hate her. I'll give her a quick one in the face.* The thoughts spun round and round faster and faster: *I'm going to kill you! She'll go down first. Go now. Can't wait any longer.*

The storm had picked up, and the temperature was falling. Visibility was very limited, and it was dark.

Ultimate Discovery

December 21. Six inches of blowing snow had fallen overnight. The plows were out before daylight, and the bus was located just after dawn. Red Bird Busing was notified, and another bus was dispatched and arrived on scene within the hour. All the passengers began leaving the bus to board the other bus except Lisa.

When the new bus driver asked Lisa if she was ready to go, she said, "We can't leave without them."

"Without who, honey?" said the driver.

"Without them." And she pointed out the window towards what looked like clumps sticking up out of the snow.

❧

8:15am. Dr. Marney Anderson sat back down at her desk with a fresh cup of dark roast coffee with two creams.

"Dr. Anderson, line 4," the intercom chimed.

She picked up the phone. "This is Marney," she said, then took a quick sip of coffee and flipped open her day planner.

"Marney, this is Larry."

"Well, speak of the devil! Seriously, what's up?"

"Well, we've had an accident over at that landfill, and the governor wants both of us over there ASAP. Three people have died from what is believed to be possibly chemical or biologic agents. He says to bring a technician and whatever equipment you think may be needed."

"We'll have to take a helicopter if we're going to be there anytime soon," she said, standing up.

"See you there," Larry said and hung up.

By the time Larry got there, the National Guard had cordoned off a mile around the area. He was forbidden to go in without Dr Anderson, so he waited at the roadblock. When Marney finally got there forty minutes later, he still wasn't allowed in.

"You may as well go home, Larry," Marney said. "You're not getting in here today. Merry Christmas."

Larry looked a little disappointed, offered the same blessing in return, and left.

Marney and the technician loaded their equipment into the Humvee, then put on full hazmat suits and drove to the site.

There was the bus, and about twenty yards further down the ditch was what looked like a memorial. They made their way through the snow and started brushing away the drifts from the figures.

Eyes glassed like marbles. Teeth bared and arms half- raised, defensively waiting for an attack. Fearful, violent expressions frozen for eternity.

The technician did a soil test, and as Marney suspected, it contained nerve gas. The German military had made tons of it between 1930 and World War II, but the science of disposing of toxic chemicals hadn't been developed yet.

Sylvester Milner, Jim Hanby, and Kristie Kittleson had caught another bus . . . with no return tickets.

Remember

That wave of liquid life that washes over you

Then drains away into eternity

A sonnet that cannot be accurately recorded

So that another may also experience it satisfactorily

It was a moment meant only for you

And the people with you

A significant event that slipped into the past

It may have been a time of laughter

Or maybe tears

All these things are stored in a treasure box

In the back of your mind

Wrapped around your soul

What is It?

I took some time to consider a thing.

A thought that interrupted my activities.

I turned the computer off and closed the lid.

I went to my room and sat down.

Contemplating this odd, almost alien thing.

A thing that doesn't belong in the natural evolution of man.

This ancient rite, this otherworldly habit.

It takes on different forms.

It can be given to a competitor but not to the vile.

You can actually add this invisible thing to another person's life.

You're giving something of yourself to someone else.

You've served them a bit of yourself.

It's something you should be careful with.

You shouldn't throw it out like confetti.

It's an ancient act.

Self-preservation does dictate a little caution,

but generally, it can be handed out freely.

The more you give it away, the more it keeps coming back.

It can come unexpectedly or even shockingly.

Most of the time it is met with openness.

At other times, it ricochets off into space, wasted.

Who can explain it?

What substance is it made of?

How is it that it can change a person's life?

Let's take a closer look.

What are we talking about here?

You wave at someone.

A pat on the back.

A soft touch.

A turning around and going back to say hello.

Saying good morning,

Wishing someone a happy holiday even if it's not your holiday.

For those that have forgotten or those that have never known.

THIS DELIBERATE ACT IS CALLED . . . A BLESSING.

Worried Robin

A robin was in the backyard, near an open window of a young couple home from work listening to the news. The commentator was going over the events of the last couple years and pointing out the gravity of the situation. The tensions between the US and its trading partners were becoming extremely tense. The war in Ukraine and the strained relationship between Taiwan and China was bringing the world to a possible nuclear confrontation. The deficit continued to rise out of control, the dollar losing to the Yuan, and there were expected food shortages coming by the end of the summer.

At this last statement by the newsman, the robin became agitated. Dropping the worm he was holding, he began hopping around in circles, chirping. The other birds came over to him, concerned, and one asked, "What's the matter, Rob?" The robin hopped over to him and screamed, "Didn't you hear? How are we going to find worms? Where are we going to go? What are we going to do?"

A sparrow who was listening from across the yard flew over and softly quoted the Bible: "Not one sparrow falls to the ground that the Father doesn't notice."

The robin quickly replied, "That's easy for you to say. You're a sparrow." Then he slapped his wing at him until he left.

Just as the sparrow flew away, a cat jumped from behind a bush onto the robin, killing it. After giving thanks, he ate the bird.

Moral: If you're okay with eating bugs and worms, then don't worry your little bird brain about where the next meal is coming from.

Dreaded Serpent

The Reverend Sven Bjordwith ended his dramatic sermon with three words: love, respect, and equality. There was a long pause for emphasis before he pronounced the word, *equality*. At which time the organist started the loud final piece meant to enrapture the congregants. After the benediction, the people began rising to exit. Two ladies hurriedly walked to the side door leading to the back hall and bathrooms. Finding their spot by a window overlooking a now vacant patio, they began their weekly gossip session.

"Donna didn't seem all that concerned that her son Gary was nearly killed in the accident, and he's still in a coma," Gloria said in a low voice, catching her breath.

Marge frowned, shaking her head. "There must have been drugs involved. How could he just turn into oncoming traffic? It shows Mrs. Reesom has a very loose grip on her children and a definite lack of discipline."

Right then, the women's bathroom door opened. Donna Reesom walked briskly out and then down the hall without looking in the direction of the two gossips.

The ladies looked at each other, and then Marge said, "Do you think she heard us?".

On her way home, Donna reflected on how she would get even with the two gossips. *I wonder what Marge would think if we told her husband that we didn't need his insurance any longer and if Gloria's husband didn't get the raise he was looking for.* The problem was that she knew Harvey was a good man and deserved a raise. He had always been a good employee at their shipping company. *Oh, what the hell, Gloria does have a point. I'm not that concerned about Gary's condition. Except for the bandage on his head, he looks okay.* She pulled into her driveway and turned off the engine. She sat there quietly staring off into space. "Gary, please wake up," she whispered. Before she got out of the car, her phone signaled a message. It was her husband, Bob. He was in China at the time of the accident and was scheduled to arrive home at the local airport Monday night. The message read, "Call me."

When Bob answered the phone, he was in flight. "Donna?"

"Yes, Bob, it's me."

"Is there any change?"

"I just got home from church. Pastor Bjordwith led the congregation in a prayer for Gary, and I'm on my way to the hospital now."

"Did the doctor say anything more?" Bob sounded agitated.

"They said there's nothing more we can do but wait."

"All the money we've spent on that damn hospital, and that's all they can tell us!"

Donna didn't respond. Her lip quivered, and a tear started to form. The silence became awkward.

Bob spoke first. "I'm sorry. You didn't need to hear that. I wish I were there."

Slowly Donna replied, "It's hard for me, too. The odd thing is . . . I feel he's going to be fine."

"I'm sure you're right. Call me when you get home from the hospital. Okay?"

"Okay. Love you."

"Love you, too."

Deep down in a darker place, a massive serpent approached the desk of Greesom, a doorkeeper. The keeper, a small, mousy man, guarded the chamber door and made the announcement for any brave visitor requesting an audience with Lord Abaddon.

"I have sssome newsss that Abaddon will be glad to hear," the serpent hissed at Greesom with a grin. The snake was still drawing itself into the room through the door twenty feet away from the doorkeeper's desk.

Greesom, shaking his head, answered with concern. "This is a very bad time to approach the master." He brushed his hair aside. "Please come back some other time."

The floor was damp with slime that made it easy for the snake to curl and slither sideways. Then he reared his head up. "I know thessse have been difficult timesss for usss." The snake flicked its tongue and disturbed some of the papers on Greesom's desk. "If I could have just five minutesss of hisss time, I think I have sssomething that will add to our sssucccesss."

Greesom believed that the slithering reptile might have worthy news, but this fact agitated him. He started fumbling with the papers on his desk while looking back and forth. Every time he looked up, he nervously brushed his long hair aside to see better. The snake was following his movements as though he would strike at any moment. Finally, the snake came up over the top of the desk and into the face of the little man.

"Jussst go to the door and announccce me."

This was altogether too much for Greesom. He looked up at the solid rock ceiling twenty feet above his head and around at the rock walls. There were only two exits: the one door was still blocked by the snake, whose body still wasn't completely in the room, and the other doors were those of Lord Abaddon. His gaze dropped to the floor. He had nothing else to do but go to the great doors.

The great doors to Abaddon's domain had not been opened for eighty-five years. The last time they had been opened, the previous gate-keeper was immediately torn to pieces. Greesom was then appointed to the position.

As he nervously contemplated his situation, more of the snake had entered the large room. It became clear that Greesom didn't have any other option. He again straightened the papers on his desk, then took two steps with a pause, then three steps, hesitating, wringing his hands, and finally, he was at the massive doors.

With both hands he took hold of the huge knocker and pulled. There was little movement. After so many years, it had rusted almost solid. He pushed and pulled until the knocker finally broke free and hit the door with a BANG! The unexpected loud noise caused the frail man to stumble backwards. He instinctively turned to run, but when he did, the snake's head was again in his face.

"Letsss try again!" it hissed.

Sweat dropped down Greesom's brow. His eyes darted back and forth. He swept his hair aside and slowly turned back to the door. He grabbed the knocker again and gave three hard knocks: BOOM!BOOM! BOOM!

A scream erupted from the other side of the door. "AAAAAAAAH! WHO KNOCKED? WHY HAVE YOU DISTURBED ME?"

The snake coiled back. Greesom froze. The color drained from his face. Resigning himself to his fate, with difficulty he managed to squeak, "Great and high one, it is I, Greesom."

"CHOOSE YOUR WORDS CAREFULLY, LITTLE MAN!"

"Great and mighty Lord Abaddon," Greesom began, trying with all his might not to let his voice shake. "The snake is requesting an audience."

"I WILL NOT TALK WITH THAT VILE THING. HIS STENCH OFFENDS ME. SEND HIM AWAY!" The doors to the great room groaned and bowed out when the lord spoke. Yellow tongues of fire licked from between the cracks.

The snake was well-known in the abyss. A patient creature of subtle craftiness, he was not equaled. He feared no one. His powerful deeds of darkness, whether successful or not, had stretched through the millennia.

Greesom was beginning to settle into his character and replied, "Great and mighty lord, please allow me to indulge your patience. He's only asking for five minutes."

There was a pause. Heavy breathing and low growling could be heard from the other side. "VERY WELL, FIVE MINUTES. BUT IF HE'S NOT WORTHY OF MY TIME, I WILL FIND MY SATISFACTION IN DESTROYING YOU BOTH!"

After he spoke, the great doors opened. Fire and black oily smoke billowed out. "ENTER IF YOU DARE!"

Greesom hid under his desk, coughing and hacking, trying to breathe the toxic air. Meanwhile, the great snake carefully began making its way into Abaddon's chamber. Once the snake's unprecedented length was through the opening, the doors slammed shut.

Within Abaddon's chamber, rotting flesh and stench filled the air. Several small fires that burned continuously provided a dim light. Black, insect-like creatures receded from the snake and up the walls in waves. There, on a ledge, was a monstrous, hideous creature. Twenty-five feet tall, Abaddon's reptilian, scale-covered skin seemed too small to enclose the muscular frame within. His head was dragon-like, with a tormented expression of fear and hate. Other disfigured creatures scurried about his feet as though tending to him.

As soon as the doors slammed shut, Abaddon in a fiery flash leaped down from his perch and seized the snake by the throat. "HAVE YOU COME TO LIE TO ME AGAIN?"

The snake, barely able to talk, said, "I didn't lie to you. They have pro…" But because of the tightening iron grip, he couldn't get the rest of the word out.

Abaddon closed his grip even tighter and yelled so loudly that the doors shook, "THEY'RE STILL ALIVE AND MOCKING ME. WHY HAVE YOU DONE THIS? YOU'VE MADE ME A LAUGHINGSTOCK AND A BYWORD!" * *see note*

At that, the great hulking mass threw the snake's head down and leaped back up to his perch, clenching his teeth as smoke curled around his nostrils. His crimson-glassed eyes showed utter disdain.

The snake, shaking his head back and forth, took a few moments to compose himself before replying. "Uriel, Raphael, and the othersss were helping them. They delayed usss ssso muccch that our time ran out and we had to return."

The dragon-like beast was quiet for several minutes after hearing the names of the beings from the other side. Finally, he said in a lower growl, "I'VE LEARNED THERE WILL BE ANOTHER DOORWAY OPENING SOON. WHAT ARE YOUR PLANS?"

The snake, finally able to speak freely, began swaying back and forth. "We've taken a different approaccch. What was united is falling apart. Absssolute truth has been replaced with sssubjective truth." He coughed and cleared his throat. "We now have sstrongholds. We have created a new ideology, and coupled with technology, it isss producccing an opportunity for your return. An entire generation hungersss for the old waysss. It will be like it once wasss. You, ssstrong one, will have your placcce again."

Abaddon was somewhat amused, but not entirely taken in. He grabbed his own head in his hands as though in pain, then thrust his arm towards the snake. "GO NOW, AND I WARN YOU, DO NOT FAIL ME THIS TIME," the beast cautioned, his voice reverberating off the walls and causing some of the insect creatures to fall off the ceiling and scurry to new hiding places.

The great doors opened, and as the snake sauntered out, its slow, measured movements irritated the great beast. Suddenly becoming wroth, he jumped down and slammed the door on the snake's tail. On the other side of the door, the snake pulled its now crooked tail through and began writhing on the floor in pain. As it curled and twisted, the serpent began to grow until it was almost twice its size.

Greesom was horrified at the sight and remained under his desk, which, as it turned out, was not a safe place. During the violent movement, part of the giant serpent's writhing body slammed against the desk, smashing it to splinters. Greesom crawled over to the wall and lay down on the floor in a fetal position.

The snake slowly regained its composure and positioned its head down to where the frightened doorkeeper lay. "Come with me."

"B--b--but I can't, who will watch the door?" he said as he sat up and backed his head against the slimy wall.

"Thossse doorsss will not open for a long time. You will come with me. NOW! Do you underssstand?"

* Note: Byword – Deut 28:37, 1Kings 9:7, 2Cron 7:20, Job 17:6 & 30:19, Psalm 44:14

Greesom's Journey

Greesom came to the same conclusion that he'd come to earlier; there was nowhere to run to, no place to hide. With the snake's head just two feet from his face, he backed tight against the wall with his head turned away from the foul-smelling creature. His response came slowly. "Yes, Master."

The massive serpent turned and began exiting the chamber. The exit led to a tunnel that gradually sloped downward. The creature looked back to make sure the little man was following. The ceiling was low, but Greesom was still able to stand upright as he walked. The tunnel turned to the right and immediately after that, Greesom stumbled over something in his path. He looked down, and in the dim light, he saw a human leg. The leg began to twitch and kick. Greesom stepped past it quickly. After a few more steps, his eyes focused on the torso of a man. The torso was headless, legless, and with the one arm it had left, it was trying to crawl up the side of the tunnel with little success. It was wearing what was left of a blood-covered service jacket. There was some lettering on the back, but it was too soiled to read. After two more steps, in the soft mud was a head. Its eyes were open and staring off wildly. The mouth moved, trying desperately to say something. Greesom knelt closer to see if he could hear what the head was trying to say. "My hat. My hat," it repeated.

Greesom had seen a hat lying by the torso. He went back and picked it up. He noticed that the words *Gate Keeper* were handwritten on the inside band. Fear gripped him again, and he wanted to run back to the gate. Before he had time to make his decision, the snake repeated, "Greesssom, keep moving!"

The slope of the tunnel became steeper. The air was warmer with every step. After what seemed to be at least two miles of walking, there appeared to be light coming in from ahead. Greesom and the serpent entered a large cave with torch lamps on the walls. When Greesom came into the room, he saw that an ogre-like creature maintained every lamp. Scattered around the room were different variants of beings including Minotaurs, Titans, fauns, and more ogres. Some of the creatures looked at Greesom, and when they did, he nervously brushed his hair aside. Most were watching the snake. Before the duo had entered the room, they could hear quite a lot of fighting and yelling among those gathered, but when the snake entered the room, all became quiet.

The massive reptile made its way to the center of the room and coiled itself so that its head was ten feet off the floor. At this height, it could look down on the entire assembly. "Asss you have all heard, we are beginning another campaign."

With that, the assembly began grunting approval and then, just as quickly, started arguing with one another.

"SSSILENCCCE!" The agitated serpent began to sway its massive head back and forth. "The next one who interrupts me again will be thrown into the fire." Suddenly quiet, the creatures stood frozen in fear. The snake continued. "Firssst, I am going to send Greesom back to the surface." At that, the snake used his tail to draw Greesom to the center of the room, making him feel even more vulnerable. "He will be my eyes and ears for the next few years."

A Minotaur shook its thick cape and scraped its hoof. It snorted loudly and glared at Greesom with narrowed eyes, then looked at the serpent.

The serpent, with red eyes glowing, looked at the Minataur. "Do you have something to sssay, Arakba?"

The bull-headed beast snorted again. "No one goes back!"

"We are now entering a new epoch. There will be changesss that we mussst adapt to. Are you going to adapt?"

Arakba stamped the ground again and boomed, "No one goes back!"

The crafty serpent didn't respond. It merely closed its eyes and remained still. Everyone was staring at the snake, waiting to see what it would do with this challenge. With their eyes fastened on the snake, they didn't notice that the Minotaur was covered with a dark fluid that was slowly draining down its body. The group turned its attention to the Minotaur when it began to swipe vigorously at the liquid. Looking down in confusion, it began collapsing into itself until all that remained was a dark puddle with two horns.

The snake began to eye everyone in the room, its satisfaction with the Minotaur's demise apparent as it swelled, pulling its head further above the group and eyeing each being darkly. "Now, are we all in agreement?" No one moved or made a sound. "Then it'sss time." The serpent, quick as lightning, grabbed Greesom's arm with the end of its tail and began to pull the small man towards him.

Mrs. Reesom had been coming to the hospital every day since the terrible accident that put her son there. The clipboard at the end of the bed offended her. G.Reesom. It seemed so impersonal. "How hard would it be to write out his full name?"

Gary had been in a coma for four days. She talked to him and sometimes held his hand, but there had been no response. The doctors told her not to expect much, as the brain damage was significant.

She took his left hand and massaged his palm with her thumbs. "Gary, honey," she said in a low voice, but loud enough for him to hear. "Sally and Mike stopped by again today. I told them that you were still resting and couldn't receive visitors yet." She squeezed his hand. "They care about you, sweetie pie."

Suddenly, Gary pulled his hand away and yelled. "No, Master!" His eyes were wild as he recoiled to the edge of the bed away from his mother, who was in total shock. The young man brushed the hair out of his eyes and, looking around, asked, "Where am I?"

Gary Reesom made a full, miraculous recovery. Things changed in his life after that. He lost interest in his old friends Sally and Mike, and not too long after that, he began dating a cheerleader. That beautiful, popular girl broke off a relationship with one of the high school football players and chose Gary instead.

Gary graduated at the top of his class and went on to the university to major in political science. He ran for city council, then mayor, state senator, and finally, after obtaining his law degree, for a seat in the United States House of Representatives. He was well-liked as a politician, but he still didn't have close friends.

During his first year as a congressman, Gary was faced with a decision that would make or break his career. The "The League for Social Justice," a radical side of the Green Party, had put forth legislation to legalize euthanasia. To be specific, it meant that anyone over the age of 70 with expensive health concerns would be put to sleep. Gary's mother was 74 and just diagnosed with kidney disease. He tried to justify the law by claiming that those people had lived their lives and that it was a burden on the rest of us to fund their care.

He climbed into bed with the issue heavily on his mind. Before sleep came, his last whisper was, "Oh, God, what am I going to do?"

When he opened his eyes again, he found that he was lying on a warm stone floor. His eyes began to focus on the lamps burning around the room. Second by second, his surroundings became familiar. Then he was suddenly hit with the reality of the place when he noticed movement through a doorway to his right.

"Greessooom" the serpent said as it made its way into the cavern.

"Master." The title came out involuntarily. He was petrified by the snake's presence.

"Are you having trouble with sssomething?" the snake said as it approached to a comfortable distance. Except for the snake and himself, the chamber was empty. The serpent tried to smile, but it was such a foreign expression for it that it looked almost comical.

Greesom was anxious to reply. "Yes, Master. There's legislation that I have to vote on tomorrow, and I don't know which way to go on it."

"Why does thiss trouble you?" The snake arched back with its head cocked a little to one side.

The man had a vacant look as he stared at one of the torches. "I don't think my mom wants to be put to sleep."

The snake was patient and let the statement linger before responding. "I'm told that the plan iss to not tell the patient sso they won't have to even ssuffer the apprehenssion of the procedure. When they go in for their regular visit, they're ssimply given a ssedative that comfortably putss them to ssleep.

"Yes, but what if she doesn't want to?" he said, looking at the snake for encouragement.

"Conssssider thisss, little one. Your mother invesssted yearsss of her life raisssing you to become what you are now. We don't want to wassste her effortsss, do we? Ssso, with that in mind, what vote would mossst benefit you and your future?"

The snake seemed to smile. Greesom did not.

Kathy Bjornestad

Kathy Bjornestad is a retired librarian and language arts teacher. She is a Wyoming Fellowship for Creative Fiction recipient, has placed in multiple writing contests, and has published widely. She is part of South Dakota's 2024 Speakers' Bureau and has four books out.

Blue Heron

What holds you to the cold October north?
   Though geese and mallards flee
   the cornfields and the cattail marsh?

   More gray than blue, a crook-necked
   ballerina frozen in *plié*—
   how long will you stand stagnant in
   the shallows while ice creeps along the shore?

   Do you love this plain so much—
   the narrow, shriveled river, faded grass,
   and pinched sky pocked with clouds?
   Tell me you will stay when all else leaves.
   Keep beside me on the river's path.
   See me through the longest night.
   Be memory of a vanished sun.

Brink

Plymouth Colony 1666

Daniel stood atop the cliff, wild grass prodding his knees. "Prudence!" he cried. A dying sun streamed around him, creating a golden aura. The wind caught his voice and cast it after her. Wavering and threadbare, it sang like bells, then sank to silence.

It had happened at the frolick, Prudence Watson thought. . . .

In September, when rolling fields, ripe with watermelon, turned gray under a tired sunset, and the full moon burst round-eyed between gray clouds. After the picking, when apple-cheeked girls and swaggering boys gathered near the bonfire on the beach, mugs filled with barley beer and heads filled with lust.

She, like the rest, had been guilty of that sin. Her eyes wandered without consent, somehow always finding Daniel Winslow. Mahogany gaze met sky-blue, shied away, then returned, a teasing dance that must eventually lead somewhere.

He was seventeen and worked for his father at the smithy. This year jutting limbs and awkward gait had smoothed into muscled grace. Prudence wasn't the only one to notice. Ann Hawkins paused to laugh and fill his cup, eyelashes fluttering. They had grown up together, along with a dozen other children, poised on the brink of the Atlantic. Prudence was one of them, yet had always felt separate, never quite fit. Her tongue tied in knots when girls spoke to her, and heat climbed her cheeks when a boy looked too long. She felt just as much as they, maybe more—all her emotions bottled and writhing like storm tide trying to escape the ocean.

The fire popped, sparks swerving past woodsmoke and heat to dissipate in autumn-tinged air. Prudence sipped from her mug and watched boys spit black watermelon seeds. She giggled when Zeb Harnell's went off-course and landed in Ann's honey-blond braids. The sky dimmed, an owl hooted, and several couples broke from firelight to claim the gathering darkness as their own.

Prudence smoothed her cambric gown, tapped a boot to John Harris's lonely fiddle, danced over melon rinds and flattened grass, past swirling skirts and dusty black hats. A curled-brown head turned her way. A hand beckoned, pulling her from laughter and light toward the surf's silver whisper. Her shoes sank into wet sand. She felt her way around boulders and over driftwood polished soft as baby's skin.

"Daniel Winslow. Are you there?"

Shooooooshhh. Water curled against her boots. Sounds of the frolick died away.

She could not see him, but the ocean's lullaby charmed her farther into the deep shade of the rocks, begged her to follow the path she thought he had taken. Did he tease? Or simply seek solitude more circumspect than other couples had chosen?

"Daniel?"

Filmy clouds moved across the moon and banished shadow. She thought of turning back but instead pushed onward, feeling her way through total darkness. Surely, he would be just ahead, waiting.

Unless it could be a trick. They had played such on her before. *Gullible Prudence. Shy and solemn Prudence. So easy to fool.* She spoke little, so her mind must be as empty as her mouth.

Yet she felt, oh, so many things! Longing filled her belly like hunger. The world called to her as the seas call to the land, a yearning that swelled like wave crests before a storm.

When the cloud cover passed, there was no Daniel, no giggling, no wicked girls, either, only lights streaming down like fallen stars. Prudence halted—unsure, confused, fascinated. Bells chimed, discordant yet compelling. She thought of witches, then demons, and suddenly wondered if she had really seen Daniel leave the frolick. Should she be afraid? The lights were too beautiful. They circled closer and closer, opened to embrace her body in a shimmering maelstrom.

After that, only ecstasy—a strange weightlessness and tickling joy which began in her stomach and funneled through weak limbs. The music crescendoed, poured down her throat and drew out mewling cries. How long did she swirl in the lights, a willing prisoner, floating like a jellyfish through a sun-sparkled bay?

She woke from heavy slumber to a memory of bells and a voice that lingered—familiar, distant, vanishing on the sharp breeze. She shook sand from her dress and returned to the fire, only embers now. Dawn pulled at the horizon, and Prudence hurried home to slip trembling into bed.

That was four months gone. All Hallow's Eve had passed, and Candlemas, too, leaving behind snowy satin blankets. Prudence had wondered at her tender breasts, the bile that rose in her throat each morning. But after several missed courses, she could wonder no more. Had it been Daniel or the lights or something different? A holy consummation like the Bible predicted. If it were, they would never believe it, not of her. She was too different to be God's holy vessel. She felt her separateness like a sin.

She went to the midwife for pennyroyal, drank it in her tea for a week and endured the bellyache. Yet the seed held, grew, quickened. Tiny butterfly kicks from the inside out.

She saw Daniel at meeting, but no secret recognition softened his dark gaze. She hid behind loose dresses and shawls, cried bewildered sorrow into her pillow.

Then came the dreams. *A firm hand catching hers, bringing her from bottomless ocean past indigo liquid to burst into sunlight. Through sea spray and heat haze a golden figure walking upon the waves.* He spoke in calming tones. Was it Daniel's voice or some spirit's? Did God seek to console her, or did a demon possess her?

Sometimes she walked the salt-rimmed cliff path, let ocean wind tug her hair loose and push at her with invisible hands. Standing near the brink, she looked down on white surf that clawed the rocky shore, its vicious power frightening. But then her gaze lifted, caught the swell of deep blue that melded into sky. That kinder ocean beckoned, echoed the voice in her dreams, whispered of a life beyond this narrow New England village.

In the sixth month, her mother caught her naked at the wash tub, glimpsed her taut, round belly and bloated breasts.

I didn't do anything! Prudence wanted to say. *It was the lights. The dancing lights!* Yet she could only stare back, wordless, until her mother slapped her hard across the mouth, and white terror blossomed into red despair.

The next morning her parents gave her over to the Elders in the courthouse, placed her before a long table that fronted the blazing fireplace. They left her standing before seven sets of coal-hard eyes, seven gray beards, seven high black hats.

Reverend Thatcher spoke. "Prudence Watson, thou hast been charged with the crime of fornication. What say thee to this charge?"

She stared past their heads, into flame, and wondered how to make them believe.

"Speak, Prudence!"

Did they hear the bells, or the whisper of oak and autumn that finally unstopped her tongue? "I did not fornicate."

"Then how do you explain the child growing within you?"

"It was the lights, the beautiful lights. They swept through me. I fell asleep, and when I woke, the frolick was over. That is all I remember."

They muttered among themselves. The reverend said, "You speak as one daft-headed, Prudence. Lights do not cause babies. You must name a father so he can share your shame."

"I know not who to name." Daniel's dark-lashed face flitted before her, then was replaced by the golden figure from her dream. Her voice shook only a little as she said, "My baby's father is the Holy Spirit."

One elder spat, "Blasphemy!" Another cried, "The girl has lost her wits!" while a third muttered, "She is possessed!"

Voices tumbled around her like poorly thrown rocks.

Reverend Thatcher said, "Prudence, if you do not name an accomplice to your sin, you will stand alone in the town square for public ridicule."

Whom to name? How to make them believe?

They led her to the platform where the minister sometimes spoke and where once she had seen a man hanged for thievery. A March wind blew ice down her back, pressed homespun cloth against her bulging stomach. She stared over the heads of those who paused to gawk and shake fingers, concentrating on the gray-sided blacksmith shop, where clanging metal reminded her of discordant bells.

Twenty days she stood on the platform for public ridicule. Then Daniel came and paused below, looking up. So handsome in green woolen trousers and linen shirt, open at the neck to show a tanned throat. She could not read his look. Had she dreamed that beckoning hand at the frolick? Did she only imagine that now he called softly, "Prudence, what do you up there? Come down." Or that his voice was the sympathetic voice of the sea?

She left the platform before the Elder came to dismiss her, followed that voice through the village. Dusk, and everyone to dinner. Smells of wheaten bread and meat broth trailed her past thatched roofs and sooted chimneys.

Up the cliff path. Fallow fields spread behind her and rocky, snow-crusted barrens before.

Westward—accusing eyes, hands that sought to mold her, restrain her, keep her from Truth. Eastward—the ocean of her dreams, hiding the hand that had pulled her upward. Maybe she could find it again.

On the precipice she stood, looking toward white-masted ships that sailed on an easy swell like plump geese. How could the Elders not believe her? How could life come to this? You were born, suckled, pulled a wooden toy across hard-packed earthen floors. Then they made you work: draw water from the well, tuck dirt around seedlings, spin flax and knead bread. Sit through interminable Sabbath meetings in a sweat-stiffened gown and admit to damnation. Recite endless Bible passages on the greatness of men, the lowliness of women. Then, when you grew too old for toys and lessons, they accused you of betrayal. Betrayed you. *Where will I go, once the babe comes?*

A sea breeze wafted toward her. Gannets cried and dove. The ocean's blue arms lulled her. She leaned forward, wanting more, needing to be cradled and protected. In a breath she was flying. Wavesong swelled. Sapphire blankets wrapped her in a glistening shroud, tucked her under and sent her careening outward on a sea of bliss.

Harbingers

Driving down the canyon where I live, I slam on the brakes to evade a puffed-up tom turkey. He doesn't seem to notice. He's *that* intent on the ladies. It's April, Season of Love for the Black Hills Merriam turkeys, and this dandy's transformation is startling. Most of the year, a quick glance couldn't tell him apart from the hens he forages alongside, but in the spring, he undergoes metamorphosis. His bald, pink head turns bluish white. A fleshy, crimson snood dangles off his beak. He fans white-tipped tail feathers, while gray-striped pinions drag a path through last fall's leaves. His black chest juts proudly, and his call, a piercing, "Gobble, gobble, gobble," carries across the valley and up into the ponderosa pines.

Hens encircle him. They pretend disinterest as they peck seeds and new-sprung grass. Another jake carries on out of sight on the hill, probably hoping for this playboy's leftovers. I slowly, almost to a stop, aim my phone out the window, and snap! Neither my obvious attention nor the rubber tread crunching gravel two yards from his forked feet fazes the vain strutter. He's oblivious to everything but the call to mate. His clownish colors, silly warbling, and ridiculously naked head make men laugh, but does he care? Oh, no. How I envy his oblivious confidence!

Ben Franklin appreciated America's wild turkeys. Comparing them to the bald eagle, Franklin declared turkeys a "much more respectable bird . . . who would not hesitate to attack a Grenadier of the British Guards." I must agree. Last year, when my dog and I came too close to a momma's nest, I was startled to see my retriever burst through the pines, chased by the angry hen. I, too, beat a hasty retreat. The turkey allowed our escape. She had only aimed to defend her nest, not draw blood from bumbling intruders.

I'd never seen a wild turkey until I moved to the Black Hills. The area is a favorite haunt for bird-hunting enthusiasts, but I prefer simply to watch these weirdly beautiful fowl, though I did once contribute to their slaughter when my husband and I encouraged our Labrador to chase a flock of striplings. The adolescents were—we thought—old enough to fly away, but our dog caught a lackadaisical wing-dragger and proudly carried it to the lip of the hot tub where we were soaking. How I regretted my role in the demise of that boneless bundle of fuzz and feathers! Though many more young birds would die before winter at the claws of fox, raccoon, bobcat, and coyote, we were responsible for *this* death. I'd thought us above the fray—benevolent gods enjoying nature's picture show. Turns out we weren't so innocent.

I don't like to remember that poor life snuffed out so easily. I'd rather recall the tom turkeys' first appearance in spring, when they are self-involved, narcissistic, and so blindly arrogant that they swagger down the middle of the road, heedless of traffic. Even a 5.0-liter V8 turbo diesel engine truck with hip-hop blaring from the speakers won't sway them. I admire their tenacity, their grit, their zest for life in this moment. Seeing them, my soul stirs. Perhaps only those of us who live in inhospitable places for seven months of the year can truly appreciate that epiphany, that moment when a proud bird reminds us that summer really will return.

Once June arrives, several hens, trailed by snaking lines of chicks, will traipse across our driveway, pause beneath the bird feeder to nibble sunflower seeds, then disappear into last year's dead thistle stalks. I love the sight, but not nearly as much as I love those motley fathers. Transformed for such a brief time, they remind me to enjoy each of nature's brief and fickle surprises: color amidst drabness, excitement amidst dullness. Before the crocuses bloom or the tulips unsheathe pink and yellow petals, these birds proclaim that warmth and new life are on the way. All is not brown, cold, hard earth. Soon—oh, so soon—sunlight will conquer darkness and reclaim these barren fields.

Hauling rock

is what I do in spring before weeds can grow.

Limestone blocks are best, especially those with

lichen dripped like paint across the gray.

I pry them loose from grudging earth.

Sometimes larva curl beneath

or tiny ants swarm forth.

I roll the rock to loosen passengers, send

it sluggish, nudging down the hill.

The smaller rocks I cradle, toss ahead.

They bounce and veer and end up

on the shoulder of the road,

so I have to gather them again.

I place my treasures in the yard

wherever weeds might spring,

assured they'll not grow

through a solid stone.

Somehow, every summer,

bindweed, thistle, grass,

find ways to cheat my sense of beauty—

the ordered bed of rock and mulch, invaded

by a stubborn spike of green.

This Old Place

I bet there are a dozen unwritten poems
   hanging around this place.
   They hide in the laundry hamper, where
   little boys burst during hide and seek to
   scatter socks like autumn leaves.
   They creep down the hallway at midnight,
   pull forth my son from slumber, sleepwalk
   him to quieter dreams.
   They sulk while I paint over handprints,
   sand dimples made by toddler spoons
   from varnished oak.
   A new house will be free of such nostalgia,
   empty as an eggshell.
   With the papers signed,
   what will become of this old place?
   Will it sing for someone else?
   Or will my memories sink like shells

into the drying creek bed
where we floated bottle caps
and hollowed out a pool
and gathered plums?

Water Music

As the first fire of summer burned low. I wondered, *Will it be the last?* Burn bans had stolen last year's bottle rockets, roman candles, and artillery shells that burst into fiery flowers. Rarely had we sat around the campfire, oozing cinder-burnt marshmallows between our teeth, or setting paper-brown leaves on the fire to see them curl into a million tiny embers. Meadow grass had given way to invasive thistle. Wispy clouds teased their way across flat blue skies, mocking us.

The winter had been cold, its snows dry white dustings that did little to feed the earth. When May came, I hurried to arrange tinder and logs inside a ring of stones, thinking, *Do it now, before it's too late!* And while the fire burned high, wafting up through box elder branches, and a squirrel growled and chittered at our invasion from a nearby limb, I tried not to imagine the pine forest reduced to ugly orange needles and ash. We'd been through a bad fire season last summer, and now I couldn't help but ponder distance. Yards from our house to the edge of the trees. Feet from the hose nozzle to the sprinkler on the roof. Length of days spent in possible exile when the call came to evacuate.

Then the first murmurs of moisture—predictions by weather fore-casters I'd learned to mistrust. *Thunderstorms.* The word rolled through my thoughts like an anticipatory bass drum.

I watched the sky. Waited. Prayed. We needed a flood to recover from last winter.

One morning in late May, I awoke to a gunmetal gray sky. Heavy fog magicked the hills into hump-backed dragons, heads tucked beneath taloned arms, mouths snorting steam. Soon the rain started, not a violent downpour with its accompanying threat of hail and tornadoes, but a steady, straight down, diamond veil.

The apple trees shivered with delight. Sprouting hosta leaves uncurled stripy hands to celebrate. Buffalo grass grew almost visibly as the rain kept coming and coming and coming.

Mesmerized, I stared out the window. I opened the door and breathed in pure summer—the smell of life and new beginnings. I nervously watched the clouds for variations in color that might signal a breaking of the storm, but Mother Nature only showered us with more, more, more.

The dry creek bed became a rushing river. Rapids waltzed past the garden and down through the trees. Water Music, as beautiful as anything Handel ever wrote, filled my ears with promise. It rained for forty-eight hours. Two days' worth. A measure like the space between despair and hope. I imagined farmers dancing for joy. I felt like dancing myself.

You never know what will happen. Life can turn to death in an instant, but death can turn to life, too. Cracked earth might grow dark and loamy. Writhing night crawlers might sprout from saturated ground, and robins might feast.

The memory of streams might metamorphose into vibrant, frolicking currents.

I had prayed, *please don't let the first fire be the last*. And the prayer was answered. Barbeque laced with thorn apple smokes on the grill, emerald hills swell toward the horizon, and summer's tapestry unfolds: a crackling campfire, bursting fireworks, and a landscape so rich with rain we might ride its bounty into August and beyond.

Margaret Bolte

Margaret Bolte retired from the U.S. Public Health Service after serving as a Commissioned Corps Public Health Officer with agencies of Indian Health Service at Toppenish, Washington, and FDA at Pembina, North Dakota. She obtained a Master of Public Health Degree from the University of Minnesota. Margaret began writing memoirs and essays after retiring in Belle Fourche, South Dakota. Her publications include *Pasque Petals* and *Scribes Valley Anthology.* She has been acknowledged by South Dakota State Fair Literature Contest for several of her stories and other writing.

A Compassionate and Caring Community

There is a corner building located off a main highway on a side street in this small, rural town in northwestern South Dakota. The sign in the large front window of this building reads, "Compassion Cupboard. Hours: Tues. 9-12 am. and Thurs. 2-6 pm."

As you walk in the front door, you enter a small grocery store. There are two aisles with shelving in the center of this establishment displaying groceries: boxes of cereal, packages of flour, salt, and sugar. The shelving along the walls contains canned goods such as beans, fruit, soup, and bagged rice and pasta. On one far wall, there is a rack containing toilet paper, deodorant, toothbrushes, and toothpaste. There is a refrigerator that stores eggs and margarine and a freezer with meat products and baked goods.

This place is more than just a food pantry. It is an active community service fulfilling a vital need. Donations of food products and monetary contributions come from local churches and community members. There is no cost for families, couples, and individuals to utilize the Compassion Cupboard. People from all walks of life use this service all year long.

Everyone is welcome. A middle-aged man, wearing a cap and a denim jacket, walks in with two pre-teen children. He shares with us that he was recently laid off from his construction job. He never thought he would need to use our food pantry. After he obtains several bags of food, we hear him say, "Once I am working again, I would like to donate back to the Compassion Cupboard." The two young daughters smile as they leave and say, "Thank you."

An older lady comes in walking slowly. Her gray hair is in a ponytail, and she is wearing a long overcoat. Every step she takes is made carefully with her cane. She shares that the high cost of medications that she needs makes it difficult to shop at the grocery store. The food she gets from the food pantry helps her so much. We ask her if she would like flour. She replies, "I don't need flour but could use sugar. And yes, I can use ground beef." Several times she tells us, "You are a blessing."

A man with a backpack opens the door and walks in. The dark-haired, bearded young man is very thin and wearing a long-sleeved shirt and faded jeans. His dark eyes are wide open with curiosity. He states that he is hitchhiking through town and saw our sign in the window.

"Could I have some food, please?" he asks. "I can only take items that need no refrigeration, for I am living under a highway overpass near the park in town." Volunteers assist him in placing canned goods in bags and provide him with personal toiletries that he places in his backpack. He speaks softly and thanks us. He leaves just as quietly as he came.

There is a lady of middle age who visits the Compassion Cupboard intermittently. She is unique in that she is deaf and mute. Communication with her is a challenge. On this visit, she grabs a grocery cart and demands her independence by selecting her own items. At times she is very forward and aggressive. We place her items in plastic bags. We give her space and treat her with respect. She is allowed to take the food she chooses; after all, she deals with her own challenges every day.

One day a young lady with three children enters and says that she ran out of food stamps, and it will be a few weeks before she can buy food. She is welcome to take what she needs. Her two girls around the ages of nine and ten are delighted to push the grocery cart; for them, it is a shopping spree at a grocery store. The kids enjoy selecting a box of cereal and getting a jar of peanut butter. The quiet mother holds onto a baby boy in her arms. Upon leaving, she remarks, "I am so glad you are here for my family."

The Lord provides. The pantry runs out of boxes of instant mashed potatoes. An hour later, a man comes in and donates six bags containing several potatoes in each bag. The man says he tries to donate to the Compassion Cupboard when he can and thought the potatoes would benefit a few families.

Two men come in with a donation of fresh eggs; 15 dozen eggs taken from their farm are given to the pantry. One of the men asks if we have empty egg cartons, as they periodically have extra eggs to donate. No empty egg cartons are found. The rancher says that they will be back in a few days to check if we receive any empty cartons. A couple hours later, another rancher comes in and asks if we can use egg cartons. He is carrying twenty empty cartons. Talk about excellent timing!

The same day, as we are stocking the shelves, we notice we are out of boxes of pancake mix. After looking in the back room several times, a volunteer notices a box placed on a lower shelf in a corner. The carton contains 12 boxes of pancake mix.

Christ said, "Feed my sheep." Compassion Cupboard is a community gift to those in need, a gift from the people of the community to the families in the community. A caring and compassionate service located in this small corner building in a small town.

Due to the pandemic, Compassion Cupboard has implemented safety measures and continues to provide essential items to families in our community. Grocery carts are filled with pre-bagged groceries to give out to community residents when they visit the pantry. Volunteers wear face masks.

The shelves remain full at Compassion Cupboard, where everyone is welcome.

A Girl Who Touched the Sky

My father was strict with his children. Being the eldest, I was always told to help my mother with my brother and sisters. Sometimes I would get away from everyone and just be free to do what I wanted to do for a brief time. My father liked to teach me new sports-related things. I think he wanted a son for his firstborn. He taught me how to throw a softball and showed me how to hold a baseball bat, swing, and hit the ball. With his guidance, I learned to ride a bicycle without training wheels. Being a tomboy, it was fun learning new activities.

When I was around ten or eleven years old, I wandered to the backyard and looked at the huge elm tree located behind our home. It was a late, warm summer evening, and this tree was 15 to 20 feet high. My mother had gone to visit her sister, my Aunt Annie, who lived next door just behind our backyard. My brother and sister were playing in the front yard. I was alone.

There was a warm breeze, and it was softly blowing the tree's big, bright green leaves and long branches. It would be fun to climb this tree and be able to look down on everything below. Under the tree, I jumped with my arms outstretched, grabbed the lowest branch, and pulled myself up.

It felt great standing on a branch in the tree! It would be cooler to climb higher. I placed my right foot on the next highest branch and hoisted myself up. Keeping the same routine, using my right foot and then my left foot on each branch was easy. It was like climbing steps on a stairway. Rising higher and higher, the top of the tree was just a foot away from me. Just one more step up, and I was high! It was awesome to be so sky-high.

The wind started blowing. The tree was swaying. The leaves made a rustling sound. Looking around, I could see our neighbors' backyards. There was my mother visiting at my Aunt Annie's backyard porch, where soft voices could be heard. They looked so small and far away. I heard other voices in the distance. My brother and sister were playing in the front yard. The sky appeared so close, and it looked so blue. A small cloud was just above my tree and me. I was high up in the sky!

Suddenly, the wind began blowing harder. I was moving with the tree. All of a sudden, my stomach got tight, and panic seized me. Feeling helpless, I could not move. How was I going to get down? I was stuck up here high in the tree! I started shouting, "Help! Can anyone hear me? Anybody?"

My little brother, Joe, heard me, and he came running. He looked so small. He shouted, "What is the matter?"

I answered, "I can't get down! I'm stuck here!"

He ran away. Where was he going? After a few minutes which seemed to last forever, I saw my father running to the tree. *Great.* I figured he was going to chew me out and ask what in the world was I doing?

My brother was nowhere to be seen; he probably did not want to witness our father reprimanding me and telling me how foolish I was to get stuck in a tree. My father asked, "What's wrong?"

I said, "I don't know how to get down from this tree!" Tears filled my eyes, but I forced myself not to cry.

It was getting windy, and evening shadows were forming; the evening was turning to night. My arms held the tree trunk in a tight hug. There was a small scratch on my right wrist and a scratch on top of my left hand. No serious cuts, though, so I was good.

My father reassured me that it would be all right. He started giving me instructions. "I'll tell you how to get down. See that branch just below your right foot? Move your leg, and just look at that branch. Put your foot on that branch. You can still hold on to the branch in front of you."

So, slowly, I started to move one foot at a time. I felt the toes of my right foot touch the branch and moved that foot onto the branch.

He said, "Next, move your left foot to the branch just below that foot." His voice was firm but calm. Dad watched me, and he would say, "Good," each time I moved down the tree. I started to feel better. He continued to direct me to each branch that I needed to step on to climb down.

One more branch closer to the ground, and I continued to follow Dad's instructions. "Use your hands and grab that low branch, and you can swing down to the ground," he said. I did. After what seemed like forever for this ten-year-old who had touched the sky and got stuck in this huge tree, I finally felt the earth. I was safe, and everything was normal again.

My father asked, "Are you all right?"

I said, "Yes."

My father did not reprimand me for doing such a foolish thing but just said, "Go find your mother." And, as he turned around and left, he had a smile on his face. It occurred to me that he probably was just as relieved as I was that I had not fallen. I was just glad that he did not get mad at me, as he usually would have asked what I was thinking to get in such a potentially dangerous position.

So, my father, who rarely showed any emotion, answered my cry for help and became my hero for that summer evening. Dad helped me, and he cared about me. It is a memory that I had almost forgotten. So many years ago, but I now remember it fondly.

A couple of years later, this elm tree with beautiful leaves and branches that reached to the sky was cut down to build an addition to our house. An extra bedroom and a new bathroom were built right where the tree had lived and where a small girl touched the sky.

Birdfeeders, Birds, And Me

Some may call it a chore or a routine task. To me, it is just something I do. No driving or traveling or making plans to reach a destination is necessary. There are no long walks. Yet, going to this place provides a sense of belonging and allows moments of reflection.

The day begins. I turn on the coffee pot waiting on the kitchen counter, glance at the outdoor thermometer, and check the weather. Then my focus narrows. It is my time with the birdfeeders, the birds, and me.

Plastic containers are placed side by side on a small table in the garage and filled with birdfeed. Sunflower seeds for the finches, unsalted peanuts for the blue jays, berries for the flickers, and suet to hang on the specified pole for the downy woodpecker.

Carrying the containers full of birdfeed, I walk to the front yard. The sky is partly cloudy, a bluish gray. A light fog is lifting, and a mist hangs in the air. The ground is damp, and the grass sparkles. The hills to the south appear dark with small patches of white snow on the peaks. There is a light breeze, and it feels brisk. No matter. The goal is to fill the birdfeeders.

As the birdfeeders are filled, a blue jay flies over me; he calls, hawking his song. Alone, I feel and hear my feathered friends. They know I am here again. The red finches are already flying to the pine trees, whistling their high-pitched notes. The crabapple bushes are quietly blowing left and right. The focal point is the sky where puffs of white clouds are starting to form, looking like white cotton balls. The blanket of mist is lifting and disappearing. The sun is trying to peek out. It will be a beautiful day.

My breathing slows. Standing in my front yard, my mind is only on the birds, the trees, and the sky. It is a time that is right now; time has stopped for a few moments. My life is intermingled with nature, and my mind is free. No thoughts of the plans for the day, the commitments and obligations, the to-do list of real-life chores waiting for me: church activities, medical appointments, calling a needy friend, visiting a sick friend, checking on family members, housekeeping tasks, etc. That is all later. Now, my attention is on the mourning dove cooing its song as she flies to the ground, and the small brown sparrows chirping as they peck on the suet. The mourning dove coos again as she lands near me. The small brown sparrows chirp greetings as they peck the suet.

I take a deep breath, inhaling the calmness and the serenity as I listen to the songbirds. It is the same every day, and it is different every day. My personal, special time with the birds and nature is a joy and a delight each time.

Walking back to my house, I hear the blue jay calling again over by the pine trees. And, in a few minutes, this majestic blue bird will fly to the feeder and grab a seed or a peanut. I turn around and take a final glance at the wide-open sky while the red and gray flickers sing their song of "rat-rat-kee" as they look for seed on the ground.

If I am capable, and God willing, I will come again. As I turn to leave, I softly promise, "See you tomorrow."

Overheard Conversations

It was a busy restaurant—a truck stop with all types of people who came in to eat a meal: local people, families, and truck drivers. There were booths to sit in and tables available in an open area of the café.

My husband and I walked into the restaurant and sat in an open booth. We ordered our lunch and received our coffee. As we were sipping our coffee, voices could be heard from a table across from our booth. Three ranchers sat around a table eating their lunch. One man with a gray cap and wearing a denim jacket was doing most of the talking. I could hear him speaking like a philosopher, and his opinions were, according to him, just plain facts.

Talking rather loudly, and being near our booth, I overheard the man saying, "The more a person works, the more money the government takes, and if you don't work, the government gives you money!" The other two men, dressed in their work jeans and flannel shirts and cowboy hats, would just nod their heads in agreement. The talkative rancher went on to say, "My son went to the University of South Dakota. Before, he didn't smoke or drink, and now in college he is drinking *and* smoking. What is that about?"

Those statements stirred a memory of long ago when I was much younger, living at home with my family. I was washing dishes at the sink. We had finished our supper, and my parents went into the living room. My little brother and younger sisters went outside to play. As I washed the dishes, I felt excited and happy. I had just had my eighteen birthday and was a senior in high school. In a few months, I would be a high school graduate. Excitement was in the air, for I was accepted into a college with classes starting that fall. The college was 80 miles from home. This was an adventure that I looked forward to.

My mother's voice was soft but clear coming from the next room, and I heard her saying, "She wants to go to that college. . . ."

Dad's voice came louder, firm yet sad. "I can't afford to send her to college. The government takes more money for taxes, and I just bought a new pickup that I'm making payments on. . . ."

"She got two scholarships to that college that will pay tuition and books, and she will have a job at the college while she takes classes," Mom replied. "We'll send her money when we can."

Dad continued, "Why doesn't she get a job at the army base where I work? She took typing and bookkeeping in high school. She could easily get a job where I work."

Mom said, "The college sent paperwork for her. They have a dorm room on campus. She'll be all right."

Dad said, "What about those parties they have at colleges? And those college boys. I just don't know. . . ."

Mom's voice was very reassuring. "We must trust her. She's a good girl. You have to let her go."

That summer I worked at Dunkin Donuts as a cashier in a town twenty-four miles round trip from my home, and my dad allowed me to use the family car to drive to and from home and work. The 1963 Mercury Meteor was red with a hardtop, an eight-year-old vehicle with quite a few miles on it, but dad had maintained it with care. I loved that car—I had learned to drive in it!

The summer was at an end, and I began packing for my trip to attend college in a couple of days. With money from the summer job, I bought some new clothes and a bright pink trunk to pack my belongings in. Again, excitement was in the air. Anticipation to start a new experience felt great.

As I was packing my clothes, my dad came to me. "Did you like driving the Mercury all summer?"

"Yes, it came in handy."

He went on to say, "You can take the Mercury tomorrow, and your mother and I will follow you in the pickup and come back home after you get settled in your dorm room. You can have the Mercury with you in college."

I was in shock! But he continued, "You have to promise me something." I looked at him and waited. "Just don't drive at night."

"Okay."

He said to write a letter to my mother every week.

I said, "Okay." We went outside to clean out the Mercury and get it ready to take a trip to college.

It was at that moment that I knew my dad had accepted the fact I was leaving home. Even though it was not that far, I would not be home every night like in the last eighteen years. My parents were strict and over-protective with us kids. Sleepovers with friends were never allowed. Our parents had to know where we were all the time. Giving me my own car was a big deal. Maybe it was just conveying a silent message that *you can always come back home using the Mercury.*

After a couple months in college, I broke that promise not to drive at night. My two friends and I were in the dorm room one Saturday evening and became hungry. One friend asked me to drive us. to the hamburger place that served terrific meatball sandwiches and hamburgers located off campus. Being an honest and still rather naïve person, I told my friend, "I can't. I promised my dad that I wouldn't drive at night."

Lillie, my friend who would have a profound impact on me my first year of college (that is another story), was an outgoing gal and fun to be with. She told me, "Oh, come on! You're a good driver. Your dad isn't here. Let's do this!"

So, we did. I drove the car that first night, and I did fine.

"Here's your order. Do you need anything else?" the waitress asked as she served us each our plate of French toast, fried eggs, and cheese omelets.

"No. Thank you, it looks good," my husband said.

The ranchers were getting up to leave their table and walk to the cashier's counter to pay for their meal. The talkative man with the cap said something to the effect of, ". . . work ethic is just being lost . . . don't know what is happening in this crazy time we are living in."

I looked at my husband and said, "That man sure had his opinions. You know, life goes on, and as they say, 'The more things change, the more they stay the same.'"

In college, I went on to graduate with a bachelor's degree in biology and sociology. My dad passed away a couple of months before I graduated from college. I think he would have been proud of my accomplishment. That Mercury Meteor was with me a few years until the transmission went out.

I never returned home to live with my parents. I would visit home on holidays and on breaks from school and work. Five years after Dad passed, my mother also died. Our family home changed forever. My mother left this world before she could meet the man that would become my husband (no, we did not meet in college). Later in my adult life, while working full-time, I received a master's in public health from the University of Minnesota. I always loved school. Work study jobs on campus provided me with spending money. Those early jobs such as a teacher's assistant to my English professor and an office clerk in the sociology department taught me valuable lessons about responsibility and being reliable. While in college, I did not go to many parties (There was no time for that!). I was too busy working and studying.

Looking back and remembering that conversation my parents had about me attending college, I realized how difficult letting me go must have been for them. Their oldest child and daughter was leaving home, and they granted me that freedom. Because of their trust and faith in me, I was able to leave my first home and find my own.

Thank you, Mom and Dad.

Recipe for Life

Practice the Golden Rule for success

Fill a cup of kindness

Stir in a teaspoon of humbleness
Blend a tablespoon of goodness
Dip an ounce of respectfulness
Sprinkle a handful of niceness
Mix thoroughly with gentleness
Pour into a bowl with heartfulness
Handle with thoughtfulness
Use with cheerfulness
Set and keep with you for happiness
Use the Golden Rule for life that is priceless.
* The Golden Rule says, "Do unto others as you would have them do unto you."

Window Blinds

We bought new window blinds for two windows in our living room, the kind without pull cords. By applying pressure with your fingers on the bottom of the blinds, the blinds could be opened, adjusted to partially opened, or totally closed. My husband was able to install two new window blinds in one afternoon.

Why are window coverings called *blinds? Blind* is an old English word meaning *to see dimly.* Our window blinds would be used to let the light in our home and when desired, block the light. At night, the blinds would be closed for privacy.

The word *blind* is intriguing. An individual who has impaired vision or is sightless is blind. Blind is also used to describe a person who is unwilling or unable to perceive or understand. As parents might say, "They were blind to their children's faults."

Hunters use a blind, which is a camouflaged covering or shelter to hide hunters from animals they are stalking.

"Blinded to the truth" is a statement heard when an individual is unable to realize or admit the factuality of a topic. During disagreements, a person may say, "How can you be so blind?" Blind in this case conveys a lack of knowledge or perception.

Blind to the less fortunate.

He was robbed blind.

Blind as a bat refers to someone who is unwilling to recognize a negative result or refuses to acknowledge the obvious outcome.

Blind hypocrisy is a phrase used to describe insincerity in heated discussions of politics and religion.

Scientists use the term "blind study" to indicate research studies of a new medication as blind, randomized trials.

Catch someone unprepared on the blind side: "Joe blindsided John, knocking him to the sidewalk."

In sending emails, a hidden, blind copy can be sent to individuals without the knowledge of other recipients. In relationships, loving someone makes you unable to see their faults: "I don't see why he bothered with her, but then, love is blind."

Today, are people blind to another's point of view? Do we have our own personal blindness to others and are therefore sometimes not open-minded?

In the Bible, Jesus compares the analogy of being blind to being spiritually lost. In Psalm 146:8: "The Lord gives sight to the blind, the Lord lifts up those who are bowed down, the Lord loves the righteous."

There is a quote: "Life isn't just about darkness or light, it's about finding light within the darkness."

The window blinds in our home will be kept open to let the light in, and at night the windows will be covered. Tomorrow the window blinds will be used again to not only bring light inside our home but to see the outside world, so we won't be blind to our reality.

Hopefully, the light will shine often so we may see.

Lynda Edwards

Lynda Edwards and her husband, Gary, ranched and farmed in Perkins County for 43 years. She began writing her memoirs after they retired to the Northern Hills in 2006. She is an active member of the Belle Fourche Writers. Her writing accomplishments include the South Dakota State Fair Best of Show (amateur prose, amateur poetry, and adult short story), Literature Sweepstakes Award, and Friends of the Huron Public Library award.

My Button

I stole a button! I was about five or six at the time. Mom and I were in the Golden Rule. The Golden Rule was a large department store that sold groceries, men's and women's apparel, and household goods. You might say it was a pre-historic Walmart. It sat on the corner of North Main.

What I remember most was the balcony which ran along the back side of the building. On one side was the office. When a payment was made, the money was placed into a canister which ran along a wire from the counter to the office. The mysterious person in the office would make change, sending the canister back to the counter by the same method. How fascinating this was for a little country girl who got to town once a month if the weather was good.

The bathrooms were located on the other side of the balcony, women's on one end and men's on the other. The bathrooms were separated by a wide hallway. A row of theatre chairs was located against the back wall. While farmers attended to their farm business, this was a common place for their wives to wait. I was intimidated by some of these ladies as they seemed so strange. They would sit with their sacks of groceries piled around their heavy black grandma shoes. When two or more sat together, they could be overheard conversing in a strange language. I later learned these ladies were German/Russian, as many had settled to the north of Lemmon.

My folks did very little trading at the Golden Rule, but I was familiar with their bathrooms. We usually purchased our groceries at the Keldron Store. This store was located on the corner of Keldron Road and Highway 12. It sold groceries and gas. We had to pass it when we went to the big town of Lemmon. My dad did most of his trading at this little country store because he could charge for a full year and pay when he sold his calves in the fall. Sam, the proprietor, did a fair amount of business with the local farmers and ranchers because he did not charge interest. His groceries were a little higher-priced, but my dad was a firm believer in keeping the small businessman in business.

After he bought the groceries, Daddy would purchase a candy bar for a treat. Daddy always had a Babe Ruth, Momma, a 7-Up Bar, and I liked a Hershey with nuts. This was the reason we had to visit the public restroom at Golden Rule. By the time we drove the 20 miles into Lemmon, I usually had chocolate smeared all over my face. Many a time Mom had to clean me up. I remember one time there was no water at the sink, and Mom had to give me a spit bath. Not a pleasant memory!

On this particular day, Mom and I were on our way out of the store when we came across our neighbor, Emma. Mom and Emma started to visit, as they had not seen each other in a while. In those days we did not have telephones. Her son, Donnie, and I were fidgeting and looking for something to do. Donnie was a year older than me and my best friend and playmate. Our families lived about five miles apart and as an only child, it was the highlight of my life to visit Donnie's family. There was always something new and exciting to do at his house.

Eventually, Donnie spied a box of loose buttons sitting on the counter. I am not sure why they were there, but he proceeded to sort through them and finally held a button in his hand. He exclaimed that he liked that one. Now it was my turn. I took the box and started to sort through it. And there it was! The most beautiful button I had ever seen. It was clear plastic in the shape of a flower, and it had a stone in the middle. I knew it had to be a diamond. What a find! It was like a rose among thorns as it sat there on top of the plain black, brown, and blue two and four-hole buttons.

Later, I remember walking down the street, Mom, and Emma ahead, still chatting. Donnie and I trailed behind looking for another adventure. I reached into the pocket of my blue corduroy pants and held out my button for a better look. I was hoping Donnie and I could compare buttons as I knew mine was the prettiest. Donnie took one look at my button and asked if my mother bought the button for me. I shook my head no. He explained to me that I had stolen the button. I had no idea the buttons were for sale. I quickly shoved the button as far down into my pants pocket as I could for fear my mother would see what I had done.

I forgot about the button until we got home, and I reached into my pocket. There it was. My lovely, lovely button. But I had to get rid of it before my mother saw it. Where would be a good place to hide it?

There it was, the perfect hiding place. My mother had a treadle sewing machine which sat in a wooden cabinet. The cabinet had three drawers on each side, and in one of the drawers was Mom's button box. I placed the button in the box. Whenever I would think about it, I would open the drawer and admire my beautiful flower button with the diamond in the middle.

Then one day the inevitable happened. My mother was sorting through her button box, and I heard her exclaim, "Where did this button come from?" I ran to where she was holding my button in her hand. She exclaimed again, "I wonder where this button came from?" I shrugged and slunk away.

I don't think I ever looked at the button again. I often wonder if my mother had any idea where the button came from. I wish I had thought to ask her before she passed away. I am sure we would have had a good laugh over it.

I have a button collection now, all bought and paid for. They are housed in a variety of jars, and they sit on the windowsill in my sewing room. Some of the prettier ones I have in a green antique canning jar, the kind that has a glass top. But none are as pretty as the clear plastic, flower-shaped button with the diamond in the middle.

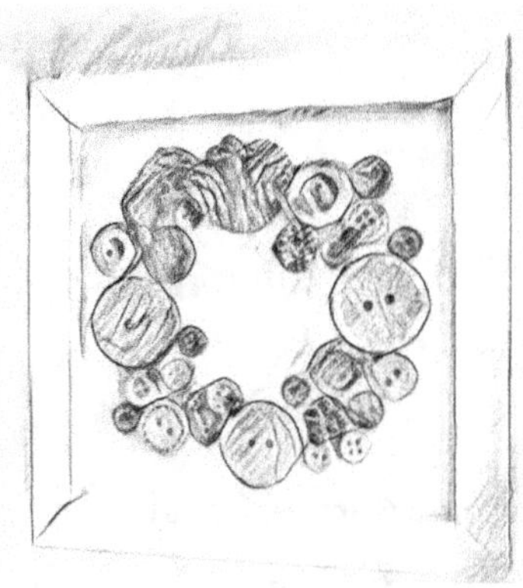

The Attic

I was hiding in the attic in hopes of escaping any further wrath from the two women in the kitchen directly below. My parents were going through a divorce. Mama had packed up, left Daddy, and moved us to live with her parents. Grandpa was in the hospital dying of cancer. The stress level was high, and tempers were short.

At the tender age of 11, I was oblivious to the emotions of adults unless they affected me directly. I do not remember what infraction I had committed. There were so many that summer. Whatever it was, it was met with a tongue lashing the likes I had never heard. Grandma led the barrage. Mama's silence was all the reinforcement Grandma needed. Grandma had raised five sons, all of whom were over six feet tall and 200 pounds. Tongue lashings were Grandma's expertise. She would have taken the gold and worn the medal proudly if it were an Olympic event.

As soon as the opportunity arose, I made a quick retreat. With my tail tucked between my legs, I snuck up the narrow steps to the attic, which had become my sanctuary that summer. It would be hot and stuffy up there, but that heat was nothing compared to what was coming out of the kitchen.

I lay down on the lumpy wrought-iron bed and had myself a good cry. When the sobbing was through, I began to wonder if anyone besides myself was feeling sorry for me. I lay there wishing someone would seek me out with a good dose of sympathy. I wanted to sneak down the stairs to see if they had missed me, but I was afraid the creak on the top step would be heard. I thought to myself, *better to be safe than sorry*. So, I held my breath and hung my head over the bed, as close to the floor as I could, in hopes I could hear what was going on in the kitchen. All I heard was the snap of the attic roof in protest of the hot August sun.

Suddenly, my ears picked up another sound. Forgetting about my sorry state, I rose from the bed. The sound seemed to be coming from the top of the stairs. Curiosity drew me in that direction, and I proceeded to investigate.

The attic was one large room with two dormer windows located on opposite ends of the stairway. I noticed a wasp doing a dizzy dance against the dormer window as I reached the stairway. I had learned a painful lesson at the age of four. You do not poke a wasp in the tail end when he is crawling up a truck window. My first instinct was to evacuate downstairs. On further thought, I decided it would be better to face an angry wasp than an angry grandmother.

I stood mesmerized by the actions of the wasp. I think I felt a kinship with the frantic insect. I knew what it felt like to be someplace you did not want to be, yet not knowing where to go.

Since I had decided not to retreat, I had two choices. I could free the poor creature or kill him. Experience had taught me that he might swat back if I took a swat at him. That left me with no other choice. I found that I could reach the window latch by standing on a box of books. Keeping a careful eye on the wasp, I unlatched the window and flung it open. At first, the wasp seemed reluctant to leave. Luckily, with the encouragement of a magazine, he flew to freedom.

When I opened the window, I was greeted with fresh air. It was still hot but a welcome relief from the sweltering heat of the attic. I stretched as far as I could and let the air caress my tear-stained face. By stacking another box of books on top of the first, I could ease my shoulders out the window. I pulled myself onto the window ledge and from there out onto the roof.

As I sat there, I had a bird's-eye view of my surroundings. Imagining myself as a large bird sitting on a nest, I felt free. I thought how wonderful it would be to fly away and escape all the injustices that had been bestowed on me that day.

In the distance, I could see a ridge of hills marking the southern boundary of Grandpa's homestead. In the thirties, Grandpa and his oldest son mined the hills for coal. It was the cash crop that enabled Grandpa to feed his family of 10 during those lean years. The mine had been sold many years earlier and was no longer being mined by the new owner. I imagined there was buried treasure in those mineshafts. I had never had a chance to search for the treasure as the grandchildren had been forbidden to ride horseback in the hills for fear of a cave-in. Yet those hills seemed to beckon me with the promise of adventure and wealth.

Directly below, I could see the backyard. I felt sad as I looked at the yellow rose bush. Daddy had taken a picture of Mama and me picking roses in June. Now it was August. Daddy was gone, and so were the roses. Somewhere in my heart, I had known that would be the last time we would be together as a family. I had overheard Grandma and Mama making plans to enter me in the rural school near my grandparents' farm. Daddy's ranch was 100 miles away, and I wondered when I would see him again.

I eased myself around to the east side of the roof. From there I could see the outbuildings: the horse barn, home to Pet and Patches, Grandpa's saddle horses; the chicken coop, no longer occupied by chickens, but by a feral mother cat and three fat kittens; and Grandpa's shop where he spent most of his time when he was healthy. Some of the family had hinted he spent most of his time there so he could smoke, avoiding the watchful eye of Grandma.

I cautiously moved to the north side of the roof. Just below was the open-air porch, where I had been caught reading Grandma's *Modern Romance Magazine*, one of my many infractions that summer. She claimed I was too young to be reading it, but it certainly had nurtured my interest in reading that summer. I found it much more interesting than my *Nancy Drew* girl detective novel.

Suddenly, I remembered it was Grandma's nap time. Grandma had a habit of taking a nap every day just after lunch. Since I was standing directly over her bedroom, I quietly and quickly hurried back to the attic. This was my chance to sneak back downstairs without being detected.

Careful to avoid the creaky top step, I started to descend the stairs. As I crept down the stairway, I made plans on what I could do while Grandma was sleeping. If I could find where she had hidden her *Modern Romance Magazine*, I would finish reading my story. If not, I would saddle up Patches, ride to the coal mine, and hunt for hidden treasures. Anything I did would be better than being in the attic if Grandma did not catch me.

The Livestock Auction

It is the mid-eighties, the cattle market bubble has burst, and prices have hit rock bottom. Banks have started to call in loans and hire hatchet men from other banks to handle foreclosures. Some families have started to relocate, moving to larger cities like Sioux Falls, Belle Fourche, and Bismarck, ND, where off-farm jobs are more plentiful. Others are hanging on, hoping for better prices. It is August. Yearling cattle are moving from pastures to sale barns.

The air hangs hot and heavy. A lone fan oscillates gently from the sixty-foot ceiling, pushing stale whiffs of cigar and cigarette smoke downward. Halfway to the floor, the air flow stalls, piling layer upon smoky layer to form a hazy atmosphere.

I am standing on the platform in the middle of the walkway which runs the full length of the sale barn. I entered the platform from the stairs leading upward from the lobby. Straight ahead, a shorter set of stairs leads down to the ground level. Directly behind me are five rows of hard wooden bleacher seats painted a drab gray. The seats are half full of a diverse group of people, mostly farmers and ranchers along with a few city looky-loos.

Some of the ranchers are young and enthusiastic about their futures, looking forward to a country lifestyle for their families. Others are old and hardened by years of hard work and failed plans. They are not thinking about the future, but hoping the present will allow them to hold on to what they have worked hard to put together over the years.

A few others stand out in the crowd, like the great-grandmother sitting on the top seat. The top seats are narrower, so she can sit with her back against the wall for support. She has her paisley tote bag perched on the seat beside her as she busily knits a baby afghan for her great-grandchild. A mother with four youngsters in tow is busy getting everyone settled. She unwraps an infant from his blanket. Taking a bottle from a tattered diaper bag, she proceeds to feed him, while the other three youngsters, all under the age of seven, look in wide-eyed wonder at the activity about them. It is obvious they are from the country by the way they are dressed: blue jeans, cowboy boots, and oversized straw hats held up by tiny ears. The oldest, a boy with a miniature rope in his hand, proceeds to practice his roping skill, much to the dismay of his siblings—his intended targets.

Below the bleachers, on the ground floor directly in front of the sale ring, a row of padded seats rises to accommodate soggy rumps softened by long hours of inactivity. Many scents like Stag, Brut, and Karate rise and mingle with the blue-gray smoke hanging overhead. These cattle buyers tap narrow white bid cards against their thighs as they stretch blue-jeaned legs cramped by long miles driven in Cadillacs and Lincoln Town Cars. Soft, uncalloused hands, bejeweled with Black Hills gold and diamonds, beckoned by a small, blinking red light. Orders are coming from Plainview, Oshkosh, and Fall River. Phones cradled against Stetson-shaded ears provide hushed, one-sided conversations.

A quiet falls over the crowd as the auctioneer enters the block. A herd of steamy-backed critters suddenly bursts through a gigantic gray door, bringing a wave of fresh, cool air with them. A rancher with a pounding heart and churning gut slides anxiously forward in his seat. Once again, the success or failure of a whole year's work lies in the hands of a few ruthless men.

The auctioneer starts the bidding. There is no response until the statistics are on the board: the number, the total weight, and the average. Then bids start coming in, left, right, high, and low. Ring men pointing sorting sticks take the bids.

Suddenly, the auctioneer hollers, "Sold." All eyes turn in the direction of the platform, curious as to who won the bid.

The bidder shouts, "Cut three back."

A moan rises from the crowd. The auctioneer agrees, and three critters are kept in the ring while the rest are headed out, flinging bits of wood chips as they rush toward another gigantic gray door on the opposite side of the ring. The bidding starts over, and three remaining critters, a rat tail, a crop-ear, and the third, sore-footed, are sold for dollars less than their herd mates.

After quickly writing something on his bid card, the buyer starts to strut across the walkway in triumph. He has saved a few dollars to the dismay of the seller. He is middle-aged, around 40 years old, with a haircut more appropriate for someone half his age. Dressed in pink shorts and a wild Hawaiian-print shirt, he does not fit the image of the typical blue-jeaned cow buyer. His sandals are more suitable for the golf course than the inside, let alone the outside, of a cattle barn. A diamond-studded earring tops off his flamboyant sense of style.

Colorful as a peacock, he struts around the walkway like a Banty Rooster trying to impress a flock of molting hens, all the time calling out crude remarks to the other cattle buyers. With a cocky smile on his salon-tanned face, he stops and turns to the crowd of disapproving cattlemen, looking for approval.

Another herd of cattle is brought into the ring, and the auction continues. This five-foot-six-inch tall,150-pound man with a tremendous case of "Little Man Syndrome," continues with his antics each time he wins a bid. He seems to enjoy the agitation he is causing the cattlemen and the other cattle buyers.

When the sale is over, everyone goes their own way. The truck drivers back their trailers to the chutes. When loaded, they hit the road and drive into the night. The cattle buyers crawl into the Cadillacs and Lincoln Town Cars heading to the next sale. The ranchers collect their checks and hope they can pay enough on their loans to satisfy their banker.

It is unknown where Mr. Flamboyant went after the sale. Most of the cattlemen and buyers were of the opinion that no matter when they saw him again, it would be too soon.

Who Stole Mamma's Onions?

About two weeks ago, something very strange happened at our house. The morning started with my mother standing at the bottom of the stairs. She hollered, "Cindy Lou, get up and get dressed, or you'll be late for school."   She does this every morning during the school week. "Amber, honey, hurry up. Your dad is waiting to take you to school."

I am Cindy Lou Bixby, and Amber is my older sister. I am 13 and in the eighth grade. Amber is 17, and she is perfect. Even her name is perfect, Amber Rose. When Mom calls her name, it sounds like a lullaby floating on a soft breeze. When my mother calls me, it sounds like she's calling the hogs. Cindy Loooou!

Amber is the perfect daughter. She is smart and popular at school. She has big blue eyes and long, wavy blonde hair. My hair is red and naturally curly. If I let it grow long, it will frizzle up when I wash it. When I tried to wear my hair long, Roger Dorsey, a boy in my class, told me it looked like I had put my finger in a light socket. So, I keep it short. That style compliments my ruddy complexion and the freckles on my nose.

Besides my sister, Amber, I have one brother. Johnny is eight years old. We get along fine if he stays out of my room. He spends most of his time in his room playing with his Batman figures.

On that morning, Amber and Dad had already left by the time I came downstairs. I was in the kitchen talking to Mom, waiting for my bus, when Johnny came rushing in. "Mom, I need a calculator for school today," he announced.

"I'll pick one up on my way home from work today," she calmly replied.

"No," he exclaimed. "I need it today!" Johnny is very excitable, and everything that happens to him is a disaster. He continued, "My teacher is going to show us how to use a calculator. We must use it to solve our math problems."

Mom scowled at him. "I don't have one. When did you learn about this, and why didn't someone let me know?"

Sometimes Johnny stutters when he thinks he's in trouble. "I-I forgot to tell you, but if I don't have one, I will get an F on my math today."

Mom sighed. Looking straight at me, she asked, "Cindy, do you have one? If so, let Johnny take it to school. I'll pick up a new one for you today after work."

How could I refuse? "There's one in my bedroom on the desk by my computer. Hurry up, or we'll miss the bus. Don't forget to close the door, or Valentine will get out of my room."

Valentine is my pet ferret. He was a birthday gift from my Uncle Jack. My birthday is on February 14, Valentine's Day. At first, I was disappointed when Uncle Jack gave me a ferret. I wanted a pet, but I was wishing for a cat or a dog. Uncle Jack owns a Pet Store on Main and 5th Avenue. He explained that Valentine would be easier for me to care for since I spend most of my time in school. Valentine sleeps 14 -18 hours a day because ferrets are crepuscles and are the most active at dusk and dawn.

Valentine has been confined to my room ever since my grandparents came for a visit this summer. Grandma claimed Valentine was stalking her. He would wait for her to come out of the bathroom and then do his Weasel War Dance. He would hop sideways, then leap and bump into nearby objects. I explained he was inviting her to play, but she insisted he was attacking her. To make matters worse, one evening while Grandpa was sitting on the couch watching TV, Valentine snuck behind the couch, crawled under one of the cushions, and nipped Grandpa on the leg. That's when Mother banished him to my room.

Johnny rushed up the stairs and came back down, waving the calculator with a triumphant smile on his face just as the bus pulled up in front of our house.

"Did you close the bedroom door behind you?" Mom inquired.

"Yes, I did," Johnny replied as he rushed out the door.

The rest of my day was normal. My friend, Cathy, was waiting for me when the bus dropped me off at school. We went to classes and sat together at lunch, making sure we sat as far away as we could from Rodger Dorsey. After class, I caught my bus and was home in 20 minutes.

As usual, Mom was in the kitchen. Since I was the first one home, it was my duty to help Mom with dinner. I didn't mind helping Mom prepare dinner because that meant Amber had to do the dishes. I noticed Mom had all the ingredients for my favorite, spaghetti and meat sauce, on the counter.

I was about to say hi when the front door slammed. Johnny rushed in and hollered, "I got an A on my math!" He flung a smudged and rumbled paper with a big red A at the top onto the counter. Without stopping, he bounded up the stairs taking two steps at a time. Mom and I knew his Batman figures were calling his name. We would not see him until dinner time.

"Your new calculator is in that Walmart bag on the side table in the hallway. Thanks for helping out your brother. He's eight years old now and needs to be a little more responsible. I'm going to have your dad talk with him tonight." Mom continued, "Honey, can you fetch me one of those onions in the pantry? They are on the floor in a net bag."

I stood at the open pantry door and looked for the onions. "Mom, there aren't any onions in here."

"Yes, there are. I put two of them in there yesterday after dinner. Do you need glasses?" she asked.

"Are you sure you put them in here? I don't see them," I replied.

"Mercy's sake, Cindy Lou, they are right on the floor by the potatoes."

I stood back as Mom approached the pantry.

"I put them here last night. I saw them this morning when I took out a new box of cereal." Mom stopped and staring at the pantry floor, then exclaimed, "Who in the world would steal onions?"

We were still musing over the missing onions when Johnny came running down the stairs. "My Joker is gone. The Joker and Batman were going to fight tonight, and now the Joker is gone." Johnny stopped directly in front of me and exclaimed, "Cindy, did you take my Joker?"

"Why in the world would I take your Joker?" I replied. I was a little upset that Johnny would accuse me of stealing his stupid Joker figure. "You were the last one down this morning. Did you take him to school again?" I asked, knowing Johnny would be in trouble with Mom if he did.

Johnny gave me a nasty look and exclaimed, "Mom, I- I didn't take him to school! He was on my bedroom floor right alongside Batman, and now he's gone."

"Maybe Batman beat him to death and buried him in the backyard," I suggested. I knew that would upset him. He deserved it for accusing me of stealing his Joker. Better yet, it made Mom smile.

"I hate you, Cindy Lou!" he called as he stomped out of the room.

"Johnny, don't talk to your sister like that," Mom scolded. Johnny was already halfway up the stairs, and I doubt he heard Mom.

Mom frowned. "Cindy, you shouldn't pick on your brother like that. You know he's serious about his Batman figures. Maybe your dad needs to have a talk with you tonight about teasing your brother."

Johnny, Amber, and I knew Dad was a pushover when it came to discipline. The three of us had yet to figure out why Mom would threaten us with that, but I knew Johnny would win if it came to a showdown between Johnny and myself. I had to think fast. "I'm sorry, Mom, but he's so funny when he's mad. You know I love him anyway."

Mom smiled, and I knew I was off the hook. She hugged me. "Maybe you could help him look for the Joker after dinner."

I nodded yes just as Amber came rushing through the front door. "Mom, guess what!"

I knew it was wonderful news. She wore a big smile, and her eyes glowed like blue diamonds. "I made captain of the cheerleading squad. Mrs. Parker said I made every move perfectly." Without pausing for breath, she continued, "Our first game is tomorrow night. I have to gather up my equipment tonight. We're going to practice right after school, and the game starts at 7. Mrs. Parker is ordering pizza, so we won't have to leave school. Isn't that wonderful? Mrs. Parker said if we develop a good routine, we'll be able to compete in the State Cheerleading Competition. I can hardly wait."

Before Mom and I could say a word, she was gone and up the stairs. We hardly had time to absorb the information when Dad came through the door with the newspaper in his hand. "Well, I see by the looks on your faces you heard the good news. She chatted all the way home. Time for some peace and quiet." Dad turned and went into the living room. He always read the newspaper until dinnertime.

It was just Mom and me in the kitchen. "Well, Cindy, since we cannot find the onions, I'll have to improvise. I have some dried onion flakes, and I'll just add some extra green peppers. You can set the table while I finish up the sauce."

I had just started placing the silverware by the plates, knife and spoon on the right side, fork on the left, just like I had learned in Home Living class, when Amber entered the kitchen. "Mom, did you wash my cheerleading socks? I can't find them."

"No, where did you leave them?" Mom answered as she added extra green peppers to the spaghetti sauce.

Even when Amber is upset, she's lovely. "They were in my gym bag with my cheerleading uniform where I always put them."

"I haven't seen them, Honey," Mom replied as she shook some dried onion flakes into the pan. The smell of spaghetti sauce was filling the room, and I was getting hungry.

"Cindy, did you take my cheerleading socks?" Amber accused.

Now Amber was not looking so pretty anymore. I looked her straight in the eye and made a face. "Why in the world would I take your cheerleading socks? Those socks are ugly!" I couldn't imagine why she thought I would even want them. They were knee-high, purple with a white streak down the outside, with the name of her school's basketball team, Shooters, written in gold letters. I didn't go to her school, and I certainly didn't want to be a cheerleader.

"What am I going to do, Mom?" she whined. "Our first game is tomorrow night. I'm the team captain. If I don't have my cheerleading socks, I'll be out of uniform."

This had to be the worst crisis in the world for a perfect, beautiful cheerleader who had just been made captain of the cheerleading team. Amber gave a little pout and waited for Mom to respond.

Mom was busy buttering some garlic toast and seemed preoccupied. "I wonder where those onions disappeared to," she muttered to herself.

"Mom!" Amber exclaimed. "Are you sure you didn't wash them?"

"Amber, if you didn't put them in the wash, I didn't wash them. Go look in your gym bag again. If you put them there, that's where they should be."

I noticed Mom was using the voice she uses when she has lost her patience. I think she was still worried about her missing onions.

Amber turned to go out the door, almost bumping into Dad as he was coming in. "Margie, have you seen my reading glasses? he asked. "I've looked everywhere and cannot find them. I'm sure I put them back in their padded case and laid them on the side table by my recliner chair after I read the paper last night."

"You have to be kidding." Mom sighed. "First my onions, then Johnny's Joker, Amber's socks, and now your glasses. If I didn't know better, I would think we had thieves in the house. But if we did, why wouldn't they steal something valuable like your TV or my new air fryer?"

Dad looked at her and smiled. "I'm sure they will show up eventually. I'll just catch the news on the TV tonight and look for them tomorrow. Is dinner about done? Smells good, and I'm starving."

Dinner was a solemn affair. Amber was pouting because she still had not located her cheerleading socks. When she wasn't glaring at me, she was twirling one piece of spaghetti around her fork. Johnny was insisting we call the FBI because someone had kidnapped the Joker. Dad assured him that his glasses had not been stolen by the kidnappers and finally forbade him to call 911 until the Joker was missing for 48 hours. Mom was fussing about the spaghetti sauce. "It would taste better if I'd used fresh onions," she said with every bite she took. I thought the spaghetti had turned out great. It all would have been hilarious if it hadn't been for Dad's missing glasses.

I was relieved when dinner was over, and I could escape to my room. Dad and Johnny headed to the living room to watch some TV. Johnny was insisting Dad should call the CIA because he was sure the Russians had taken the Joker. Dad was getting a little irritated with him and insisted Johnny should just be quiet and watch *Gunsmoke*. Amanda was still fretting about her missing socks all the time she was rinsing dinner dishes and loading the dishwasher. Mom was on her hands and knees, busy cleaning out the pantry just in case the onions were hidden under something.

I was looking forward to playing with Valentine because this is the time of the day when ferrets are the most active. When I opened the door, I knew he would come out of hiding and start his Weasel War Dance, his invitation to play. I ascended the stairway as fast as I could without running. Running in the house was forbidden, except for Johnny, who ran every place he went. I guess this is expected of eight-year-old boys. At the top of the stairs, I turned right and headed down the hall to my room. I turned the doorknob and opened the door just wide enough to enter. I quickly shut the door behind me in case Valentine was hiding and tried to bolt out the open door.

I waited a few minutes for Valentine to come out of hiding. When there was no response, I quietly called, "Valentine, where are you?" I suddenly started to feel apprehensive when he didn't respond to my voice. I stomped my foot and shouted, "Valentine, it's time to play!"

Now I was really scared. I started to look in all the places Valentine liked to hide: his cage, under my bed, and in the corner of the closet under the pile of clothes he liked to burrow under. When I could not find him, I looked under the pillows on my bed. When he was not there, I realized the thieves had taken Valentine along with Mama's onions, Amber's sock, Dad's glasses, and the Joker.

I ran down the hall to the top of the stairs and hollered as I made my descent to the kitchen, "Mama, the thieves have kidnapped Valentine!"

Mother stuck her head around the door. "Did you forget to close your bedroom door again?" she asked accusingly.

"No, the door was closed when I went upstairs. I looked everywhere, and he's not in my room."

By this time Johnny, Dad, and Amber had joined us in the kitchen. Johnny was excited, and he insisted we should call NCIS, Los Angeles, in case terrorists had taken Valentine. He ran to get the phone, but Dad stopped him before he had a chance to dial. "Now, let's calm down and think about this. It makes no sense that thieves would break into our house, and all they took was a pet ferret, my glasses, and Amber's socks."

Johnny interrupted him before he could finish. "The Joker! Don't forget about the Joker!"

"Yes," Dad agreed. "We can't forget about the Joker. There's not a thing we can do about it. Let's go into the living room and watch TV." TV seemed to be Dad's solution to all his problems.

We took our places in the living room: Dad sank into his recliner, Mom picked up her embroidery as she sat down in her chair, Amber and I took up opposite sides of the couch, and Johnny sprawled on the floor with one of his Batman figures. Reruns of *Family Feud* were just starting.

Steve Harvey had just finished introducing the Hall Family when a brown streak ran across the floor and disappeared.

"Valentine!" I shouted as I dashed to where he was hiding. He had ducked under a quilt that was hanging on a rack in the corner. I lifted the quilt and was greeted with a loud hiss, which ferrets do when they're scared.

"Poor little fella," I cooed as I gathered him in my arms, accidentally pulling the quilt onto the floor. "How did you get out of my room?"

Mom let out a gasp. "You nasty little thief. Shame on you!" she exclaimed.

We all looked at her, wondering what she was talking about. Then we saw it. Lying on the floor under the quilt rack were all our stolen items.

Dad started to laugh. "The mystery has been solved. You know, I just remembered that the name 'ferret' is derived from the Latin 'furittus' meaning 'little thief.'"

With Valentine in my arms, I had started up the stairs when I spied the new calculator on the side table in the hall. Everything became clear to me.

Valentine had slipped out the door when Johnny had gone into my room looking for the calculator.

I thought to myself, *Valentine must have been remarkably busy today living up to his name, "Little Thief."*

My South Dakota Home

When dusk descends on the Dakota plains,
a metamorphosis takes its place.
The hot summer wind calms to a whisper.
The faint scent of sweet clover drifts
on a cool evening breeze.

Pronghorn antelope rest among sagebrush on native
grasses.
Whitetail and Muleys abandon their wooded hideaways
to seek dew-kissed alfalfa leaves.

As twilight begins to dim, turkey buzzards roost on lofty boughs.
The magnificent eagle makes a final swoop
before resting on a rocky ledge.
As the shadows lengthen and darkness falls,
barn swallows retire to their mud-thatched condos,
replaced by barn bats, gliding silently in the evening sky.

The night is held in a black void,
until the silence is broken by
the proverbial question of the night owl.
A lone coyote on a nearby butte
answers with an acapella call to its mate.
The bullfrogs in Whitney Creek provide
base and baritone harmony,
while crickets sing a melancholy song.

The night awakens with the sweet music
of My South Dakota Home.

Night Watchman

Fully dressed I stumble
   for my makeshift bed.
   Wavy black and white lines greet me,
   TV station, long gone.

   I grope in the dark
   for leather gloves and flashlight.
   Donning overalls and boots,
   I start my 2 AM check.

   The dark night slaps me awake
   with the strong smell of thawing manure.
   As I cross the rutted road,
   my booted feet are greeted
   by the crunch of breaking ice pockets.
   Trekking from the house to barn,
   darkness surrounds me,

holding me in a silent void.

The moon is playing hide and seek
behind a layer of wispy clouds.
The stars are so high,
they don't bother to twinkle.

My alert ears pick up
the sound of a thawing creek.
The forlorn hoot of a night owl
travels faintly on the chilly breeze.

The eerie yipping of coyote pups
sends a shiver up my spine.
I hasten my pace.
I reach my destination,
a wall of whitewash boards.
The corral gate squeaks.
A herd of black heifers
move nervously at the sound.

The dim beam of my flashlight reveals
switching tails and frosty breaths.
I proceed with caution,
no sudden movement.
Circling the corral, my flashlight
moves from side to side.

I methodically cast my light

over each and every body.

Searching, searching, searching.

At last, at beam's end,

a miracle appears.

A slimy, slippery baby.

A tender, caring mother.

Another sign that spring has arrived.

Prairie Playground

As a child growing up on the prairie plains,
  I played beside the old, abandoned sheep wagon.
  A shady spot: a resting place for me.
  Herd of stick horse mares and colts,
  remnants of the cedar fencepost pile.

  Riding upon my favorite mop handle stallion,
  I raced like the wind through cactus clumps
  until my long hair was like sagebrush snarls
  and my cheeks were dry as hard-pan spots.

  Tired, I sat against the wooden wheel and spoke,
  resting among my wild herd.
  I listened to the sun-bleached canvas
  fluttering in the hot summer breeze.

  Dizzily, flies buzzed above my head,

then darted back to the fresh cow pie.
Rested and refreshed, curiosity drew me
to the sagging wagon door.

There was only a broken, rusty latch
between me and the treasures within.
Peering inside, I was confronted by
hot, musty air and spiderwebs.

Suddenly, from the depth of the darkness,
I imagined a ghostly voice warning me to
"Go away . . . go away."
Fearfully, I raced toward home,
leaving my wild stick horse herd
in the care of the sheepherder's ghost.

Scattering Ashes

Scatter my ashes into the wind.
    Let it carry me to places I have never been.
    If I am dropped upon a warm cow pie,
    I can sleep by echinacea pink and high.

    If I am cast upon the water, cool and clean,
    I will watch little boys catching frogs
    as I am drifting down the stream.

    If there is a city sidewalk near a pile of rocks,
    there I'll lie listening to laughing little girls
    playing hopscotch in their frilly frocks.

    If there is no wind, then scatter me
    near Whitney Creek, a deserted place
    where the old folks used to be.

It is a peaceful prairie place I've often seen
where Mamma Mallard calls softly
To her ducklings drifting on the stream.

When nighttime casts a shadow long,
beneath a moonlit sky, the silence breaks
when coyote pups sing their eerie song.

Let my ashes lie beneath that willow tree,
where I will wait for a gentle breeze
to lift and scatter me into the winds
to carry me to places I have never been.

The Girl in Skin-tight Jeans

When I was young and in my teens,
I liked to wear skin-tight jeans.
Now that I am old with flab,
clothes with comfort are what I grab.
When I was young and in my teens,
I noticed boys far, near, and in between.
Now my sight is growing dim.
Hard to tell if it's her or him.
When I was young and in my teens,
there was a future in my dreams.
Now that I am old and fading fast,
all my dreams are of my past.
No matter what life brings today,
at night it goes away.
I feel young again, or so it seems,
dreaming of that girl in skin-tight jeans.

The Shack

The toilet, the biffy, the hooter, the can.
  They are the same, no matter the name.
  Refers to the little wood shack
  at the end of the path, which leads out back.
  No matter what it's called, it's a handy place
  for the urge, the purge, or sitting in solitude.
  Many leaf the catalog through,
  and some like to smoke while they do.
  A moon-shaped window on the door,
  wooden boards make up the floor.
  One hole, two holes, or three,
  depends on the size of the family.
  Some had Sears and Roebuck on hand.
  You are lucky to find Charmin in a can.
  If not, a corn cob would do,
  although rough on a hemmie or two.
  Most are occupied by spiders and flies

and the occasional snake.

When he comes around,

a quick trip you will make.

When the wind does blow and the night is black

and there is a breeze in every crack.

You hope you don't have to make the track.

Best to take your time going, but hurry back.

When you sit there in the breeze,

unmentionables below your knees,

your nose is running, and you start to sneeze.

All those fun things will have to wait.

No time to read, smoke, or cogitate.

Sometimes tipped over, but never tipped back,

A victim of many a prank, I think.

In the morn after Trick or Treat, pity the man

to find his place of refuge on the brink.

Today, most are sorry and dilapidated,

replaced by port-a-potty or porcelain throne.

Since we love our modern conveniences,

the poor old shack we do not mourn.

The Sheepherder's Courtship

The old sheepherder decided to date the widow down the way
   when she caught his eye at the feed store just the other day.
   He'd been divorced for three-plus years, she widowed about the same.
   She already had several suitors, so he'd have to play the dating game.
   Suitor number one plowed her fields with his tractor, green and big.
   Suitor number two, a party man, liked to drink, laugh, and dance the jig.
   Now the sheepherder did not have a tractor, which was a shame.
   Dancing was not his style as his old left foot was pretty lame.
   So while he smoked his pipe, he plotted out a plan.
   With something that could not be beat by any other man.
   He heard the widow had a band of sheep she loved so dear.
   What he did not know about those woolies would fit his ear.
   So he dressed in his Sunday best with court'n' on his mind.
   With a smile, she met him at the door. She was a friendly kind.
   Over coffee, they chitted and chatted the whole afternoon through.
   He suggested if he saw her sheep, he could give a tip or two.

They drove the pasture in her pickup looking for that flock.

When he saw that band of ewes, he had a terrible shock.

They had tags, and ticks and maggots, spoiled bags at the best.

He knew this sorry mess of ewes had put him to the test.

Now he was a truthful man and could not tell a lie.

What he had to say would make her cry.

Much to his surprise, she fired up at what he had to say.

Without a second thought, she told him, "You best be on your way."

As he drove down the road in his trusty Jeep,

She shook her fist and shouted, "Love me, Love my sheep!"

Now the sheepherder would do anything for love,

but what that widow asked was way above.

It galled him to admit he had met defeat

to that widow's little herd of sheep.

But it would take more than that to knock him down.

Just to prove a point, he'd marry that redhead in yonder town.

He knew she had five kids he would have to keep,

but that was better than a raggy taggy band of sheep.

Meg English

Meg English is a South Dakota native. She and her husband of 43 years, John, have a home in the South of France, but Meg likes to drift back to the Black Hills for extended stays. Meg taught high school in Minnesota, Wyoming, and South Dakota. She has a BS in English, an MS in history, and an Ed.D. in educational administration. She currently writes for the Belle Fourche *Beacon*, enjoys her nine grandchildren, and continues to develop her skills as a watercolor artist. She has attended all public colleges in South Dakota.

A Question of Vermin

Rick and Temple Green were enjoying a quiet summer morning on their garden patio. A leafy basswood tree provided just the right amount of shade. The garden was blooming with climbing clematis, hearty Russian sage, hanging baskets of petunias, and leafy groundcover.

"Look at this," Rick said, holding up a newspaper for Temple to see. "Isn't this the place where your Aunt Jenny works as a hospice volunteer? Alcott Estates Assisted Living Residence in Canyon Hills?" Rick indicated a front-page photograph of a sprawling modern building with a red tile roof, landscaped with greenery. The sky was bright blue and cloudless. The news heading read, "Alcott Estates Resident Succumbs to Poison Spider Bite."

The headline evoked a chuckle from Rick. "Guess you can never be safe from spiders. Probably a good way to go. Says here the victim was Dr. David Thorndyke, 85," Rick mused as he referred to a small inset photograph of Dr. Thorndyke.

Temple leaned forward to regard the photo of Alcott Estates and the headshot of an elderly man. "Nice Photo-shop work," she commented on the unrealistic greenery. "Alcott Estates is on Poison Spider Parkway. Nothing grows out there. I've been there a couple of times with Jenny." The photo of the man, Dr. Thorndyke, was unremarkable to her. His eyes squinted as if looking into the sun. Thin wisps of hair were arranged over a balding scalp, and a fine, trimmed beard covered a nondescript face.

"How is Aunt Jenny?" Rick asked, diverting Temple's attention from the newspaper images. "Haven't seen much of her these past few months."

"She's fine, I guess."

Temple felt a sudden twinge of remorse, or more specifically longing for her aunt. Aunt Jenny, her mother's younger half-sister, was only nine years older than her. From the time Temple could walk, Teenager Jenny had been her babysitter. They had had many adventures. Sometimes they crossed busy streets with Jenny holding tightly to her small hand. Jenny was Temple's first teacher. Jenny had taught her jump rope rhymes and how to ride a bike. It was Jenny who bandaged the knees and elbows. Jenny introduced her to the public library, taught her to read her first words and how to imagine stories. Then Jenny went away to college, bound for law school.

Eventually, Jenny had come back. She lived alone in a comfortable bungalow with a gray cat and a pristine garden, not more than a thirty-minute drive from Temple's and her husband Rick's comfortable home.

Aunt Jenny had recently retired. These days, Jenny could often be found on her knees in the dirt, cultivating plants, garden claw in one hand poised to control outlaw vegetation. Her career as a tireless public defender and champion of civil rights was now set aside for a well-ordered home.

"Good God!" Rick lamented, moving on to the next article. "The Feds are talking about raising interest rates!"

While Rick began his own dialogue denouncing the misguided direction of the Federal Reserve, Temple reached for her phone to extend an invitation to Aunt Jenny. It was overdue.

Later that evening, Jenny responded. "Great to hear from you, girl! Just got your message."

"Hi Jenny! It's been too long. We miss you." Temple began to describe her plan for a family barbeque, but Jenny diverted her mission. "That would be fun, Princess, but maybe later in the summer? I've been awfully busy. I've absolutely decimated the attic. Isn't it incredible what you can accumulate?"

Temple's mind shifted to Jenny's passion for thrift stores and yard sales.

". . . and there are some things I've set aside for you to look at. Would you come over to see what's here? You don't have to take anything if you don't want it. How's tomorrow sound? Around 10?" Jenny always had a plan, or so it seemed to Temple.

Jenny's pretty silver hair was arranged in a tight ponytail when she greeted Temple the following morning. Jenny, always immaculate, wore eyebrow pencil, perhaps more than what might be considered necessary, and an attractive shade of pink lipstick. Temple enjoyed the warmth of Jenny's tanned skin as they embraced

"Girl, it is so good to see you! I made tea, my own herbal specialty with mint, blueberries and a few other things that seem to work together." She led Temple from the cloistered, old-fashioned foyer to the open kitchen. The gray cat trailed silently behind, tiptoeing, tail waving.

Jenny's authenticity was a familiar comfort to Temple. The mingling herb odors, something cooking, the earth tone décor, and unusual collections were Temple's symbols of safe, sweet, innocent childhood.

A good thirty minutes passed as they caught up with news. Were Rick's three teenaged children staying with them for the summer? What would Temple be teaching in the fall? Local politics, the benefits of yoga, and must-read books also entered the conversation.

"Rick and I have been wondering," Temple said, recalling the newspaper article and the photograph of the sprawling Alcott Estates with its faux greenery, "Are you still doing volunteer work there?"

"Hospice volunteer work is therapeutic, until it isn't," Jenny reflected with characteristic obtuseness. She poured another cup of tea for Temple and some for herself. "Here, Princess, have another scone. They're small." Temple helped herself to a "small" and delicious homemade scone after she cut one in half with a sterling silver butter knife. Jenny's scones were never small.

"Rick showed me an article in the paper about that guy who died from a poison spider bite at Alcott Estates. Did you know him?"

"Spider bites are very common in Colorado, and all spiders are poisonous," Jenny said as she took a small bite of scone followed by a sip of tea. "However, if we are referring to the same situation, the victim didn't die from a simple spider bite." She brushed some scone crumbs from the table into her left hand and emptied them on the serving plate. "It just looked like one."

"Well, then how did he die?" Temple's curiosity was piqued.

"I killed him," Jenny said, looking straight at Temple.

Several moments of stunned silence passed before Temple found the breath to speak. "Jenny, for a minute there, I thought I heard you say, 'I killed him.'"

Jenny looked down at her long, slender fingers and manicured, oval-shaped nails. Genteel hands that were also capable of hard work. "Yes, I did say, 'I killed him,' didn't I? What was I thinking?"

Temple, a high school teacher and wife of a circuit court judge, was incredulous. She waited for Jenny to laugh or smile, to know that the Jenny with her tongue-in-cheek sense of humor was only joking.

"I'm so sorry, Princess. I shouldn't have said that. It slipped out. Remember when you were small, and I took care of you? We had such fun! Remember when you were only three or so, and I carried you on my back, and we pretended that we were running away from insane, possessed lawn mower operators at City Park?"

Temple remembered and managed a smile.

"As you can see, there's a lot of work in downsizing. You certainly don't have to take any of these things if you don't want them."

Temple nodded, waves of emotion taking over. Hot tears formed in her eyes.

"You know, you can help me rummage through some memorabilia, and you can decide what you want to keep or not, if it's not too late."

You just never know what you're going to find when you clean out your attic.

The attic was a repository, an organized, clean collection of memorabilia. It smelled of wood, dust, and paper. Old paper. The air was hot here at the top of the house even though shaded by leafy sycamores.

Two black filing cabinets stood tall against the walls on either side of the south-facing attic window. Jenny approached the left-hand side cabinet and sat on the wood floor. She tugged on the bottom drawer which made a certain metal screeching sound as it opened. "Drat," she said. "Maybe a shot of WD-40 would help. I hate to have to get a new filing cabinet and transfer all this stuff," she said while Temple sat on a cushioned footstool.

"Here, you can put this on top of the other cabinet for refiling." Temple stood and handed several school notebooks to Temple.

"Here's Exhibit 1." Jenny pulled out a resistant hanging file folder, neatly labeled, "High School Icky Stuff." A group of glossy 8 x 11 closeup photographs dropped on the floor. Jenny picked up the top photo and handed it to Temple. It was a photograph of a tame white rat with dark gray markings. The rat was not altogether reprehensible in the photograph. Temple could see the little claws, the whiskers, the small ears and the bright little eyes. As rats go, it was not unattractive altogether although the long, hairless tail was off-putting.

"That's Mightas," Jenny explained. "We had two rats in the biology lab at high school. Do you remember Marcus Welby from the television series, *Marcus Welby MD*, with Robert young? We used to watch the reruns in the late afternoon. We'd just got cable. Then, after *Marcus Welby*, your mom would pick you up."

Temple vaguely recalled the show.

"Anyway, I named the rats Marcus Welby and Mightas Welby. Mightas Welby was the female," Jenny added. "Poor Mightas had babies. They were so tiny. She must have given birth at night. One morning we found five dead babies, their tiny tummies eaten clean out. You could even see what was left of their little ribs. We blamed Marcus and decided that if there were future babies, we would have to separate them. So, when it looked like Mightas was pregnant again, we moved Marcus to his own cage. And guess what? The same thing happened. The babies were born one night and reduced to carnage by the next morning."

"So . . . what happened?"

"Well, Mightas was clearly guilty, and apparently cannibalism is not uncommon among male and female rats in captivity. Given that about half as many of the babies were consumed the second time, maybe Marcus was also guilty."

"Did you kill him?"

"The rat?"

"No, Dr. Thorndyke, for God's sake."

Jenny continued, "It's important to note that the Welbys were not great parents, and this is all part of the story that begins to address your question.

"You see, in high school, I was the biology lab assistant, hand-picked out of all the sophomore students. I was so honored." She picked up the pile of fallen glossy prints. "Here's one of me." She handed Temple a photo of a young teenage girl with long, curly black hair, faded denim jeans, and a peace symbol t-shirt. The girl held a white rat with a tan strip of color down its back and head, Marcus Welby. Just behind her was a tall man with a beard and glasses, balding and wearing a leisure suit jacket. "That's my teacher, Dr. Thorndyke. He chose me to be his lab assistant." Temple felt Jenny's eyes on her. "There were more capable biology students among the sophomore class, I can assure you."

A small child with curly black hair stood beside Jenny. Temple stared at the black and white photograph. Clearly, that was a photo of herself at about age five. She had a vague memory of accompanying Jenny on a visit to a large school building after school let out or maybe in the summer.

Temple was stunned yet again.

An older man, a teacher in love with a high school student, a child. Temple understood. As she studied the photo of Marcus Welby and Sophomore Jenny with Dr. Thorndyke, the human perpetrator, lingering in the background, Temple shivered.

Her beautiful Aunt Jenny, a murderer. But justified, perhaps, because another crime had also taken place.

"Would you like to sit down, my dear? It's all a lot to take in," Jenny said. Temple sat down on a chair in the attic room.

"Dr. Thorndyke said he loved me. He wrote me poems about our love."

"Jenny, this is so creepy. I'm stunned," Temple said. "I'm angry!"

"Yes, creepy. And I'm angry, too. It came to me during a series of epiphanies over the years. He used to write notes on my notebooks, like the ones you handed me. I was so flattered. I was only 16, desperate for attention, but that's another story."

Temple remembered a notebook with a frayed cover in her hand and put it down. She didn't like the feeling of holding it.

"Did anyone else know, Jenny?" Temple asked in a whisper.

"I've often wondered," Jenny said. "Yes, I think so. But even so, you can imagine the repercussions even then. It was not something to be discussed openly."

"But Jenny, tell the truth. Did you really, well, *kill* him?"

Jenny smiled her warm smile and brushed a shock of Temple's curly hair off her face where it had fallen. "Figuratively, yes," she said. "I've been killing off the memory for years. Washing my hands, like Lady MacBeth. It's satisfying and freeing. I keep this folder, "Icky things from high school to remind me not to forget." Jenny paused. "Forgive but never forget," she said.

"What this guy did to you is unconscionable! How could you possibly forgive?" Temple asked.

"Not him, dear. I have forgiven myself. Let's go out to the garden." Jenny took Temple by the arm. "I'll show you where I buried the evidence. Oh, and here's a fun fact! The deadliest poison spiders are found in the Black Widow phylum. I learned that in sophomore Biology class."

PrIncess "I"

Once upon a time there was a princess with long blond hair who liked high-heeled shoes and pretty dresses. The princess had lovely clothes, certainly more clothes than one person could ever wear in a lifetime.

Her shoe room needed no special lighting, as the shoes created their own brilliant chromatic display. The princess owned yellow shoes, red and purple shoes with pink bows, striped shoes, and even shoes with red, blue, and white polka dots that she wore to the annual 4th of July Parade. All the beautiful shoes had spiked heels, and the princess kept them all lined up on the shoe shelves in her shoe room in no special order.

The princess also had many splendid dresses. There were long ones, short ones, blue and red ones, and one to match every pair of shoes as well as quite a few flowing gowns with silver and gold sequins. Of course, there were matching handbags, jewels, and lots and lots of earrings.

Her hair was so long that she could sit on the ends if she wanted to. Sometimes she wore her hair up, and sometimes she wore it down. And several times a year, the royal plumber was summoned to remove hair from the castle plumbing.

The princess had a very long name. She was called Isabella-Janine-Porta-bella-Portia-Petunia-Ophelia after her royal grandmothers Isabella and Janine, and her royal great-grandmothers Portabella, Portia, Petunia and Ophelia. The long name was much too hard to remember, so everyone called her PrIncess I, for short. The capital I in her name was added to distinguish her from all other princesses who might try to impersonate her.

Unfortunately, the princess with beautiful shoes, glamorous dresses, and splendid long hair had a reputation for being extremely untidy.

There were bits of bacon and leftover fruit salad and bowls of gravy turned to muck under the princess' bed. Instead of tidying up after herself, PrIncess I piled her purple monogrammed flannel blankets higher and higher on her bed so she could perch near the ceiling and escape from smelly socks and other disgusting things below.

The royal housekeepers were afraid of what they might find in the princess' chambers, and so they threatened to leave for another palace. "We are leaving," they said one day, and they marched off one by one out the castle door, across the moat and off to the next castle, vowing never to return. PrIncess I was not even aware that they had left. She rather liked her chambers as they were.

The next day, when her mother, Queen Petulenta, PrIncess I's royal mother, was passing by PrIncess I's chamber door, she caught the perfume of something quite disgusting and was stunned by the foul odors. She nearly tripped over a collection of dirty dishes and cutlery the princess had left outside, unaware that room service staff had fled the castle.

Queen Petulenta appealed to the king. "The Princess lives in squalor! The royal housekeepers have left and won't return! What are we going to do?" The queen wailed.

"I wouldn't worry about it, my dear. She'll get around to cleaning eventually," the king said.

"But she's 27 years old!" her mother declared.

"She's *only* 27 years old!" Her father sighed. "Soon she will marry and go away forever." And he seemed quite sad. "I will speak to her," he promised.

The very next day, the king met PrIncess I at the Country Club for lunch. "Princess," he began after they had consumed a sumptuous vegan feast of walnuts, cranberries, kale, and gorgonzola. "I have been meaning to talk with you about your future."

"Yes, of course, Father." She fixed her lovely gaze on him and leaned forward to listen.

She was so pretty. The king felt his heart melting, and he almost forgot what he had been sent to talk to her about. "Well, my dear, I am . . . I mean your mother is . . ." He stumbled for words. "I mean your mother and I are very concerned that you will never find happiness in marriage or . . ."

"I don't want to be married, Father."

"Yes, of course." As usual, the king did not know what to say next. And so, they discussed trivial things and went home to the castle where the queen was sitting in the parlor, and PrIncess I went to her room where she stayed up all night and slept all the next day. Queen Petulenta was more distraught than ever, and even the king was a little annoyed, perhaps with himself.

Little did they realize that something was about to change. A powerful, magical barista had overheard the king and queen's conversation and Queen Petulenta's plea for help.

The next afternoon, when she woke up, PrIncess I went to Starbucks and ordered a double latte with low-fat milk, no froth, and chocolate sprinkles in a biodegradable paper container with a wooden stirring stick. A little wizened man in a green plaid vest with a white polo shirt took her order.

"Congratulations, PrIncess I!" the little man sang as he prepared her drink, making sure to *froth* the milk and *omit* the chocolate sprinkles.

"How do you know my name?" she asked.

"I am a barista, my dear, and I know everything about you! You are our lucky 15 zillion millionth customer!!!" He smiled, revealing a gold front tooth. "If you can answer one riddle, you will be the lucky winner!"

PrIncess I thought the little man was very strange, and he was. His skin was wrinkled, and he wore white even though it was past Labor Day.

"OK. What's the riddle?" she asked, stirring her coffee. "Hey, what happened to the sprinkles?"

The strange little man pulled out a pair of glasses from his vest pocket and slowly read the question on a scroll that appeared from nowhere. "How many I's are there in princess?" Before she could respond, he blurted out "Only one!" And the little man burst out laughing. He wiped a tear from his eye and laughed again. PrIncess I didn't laugh. "Don't you get it? I mean, only one I! Don't you GET IT?

The princess was nonplussed.

"Seriously, as our 15 zillion millionth customer, you have won a *free* pass to the Better than Nothing Improvement Day Spa!" And he flashed the gold tooth smile.

"Is that even a real number?" PrIncess I started to ask, but the strange little man cut her off.

"Hmmm . . . Are those split ends, Dearie? We'd better get busy! No time to waste in your case."

The funny little barista man grabbed her arm and pulled PrIncess I behind a dark curtain that appeared out of nowhere before she realized what was happening.   The princess went to the spa, but as anyone who has ever read a fairy tale knows, the spa was merely a ruse. It was really a school for practical living and good behavior. PrIncess I found herself sitting on a plastic lawn chair as a team of improvement specialists set about their work.

"Ewww, plastic lawn chairs!" she complained.

"Here, Dearie, put these on." The strange little man handed her a pair of yellow rubber gloves.

"These are pretty," she said, "But I don't like the way they fit."

"The better to protect your pretty hands," he said.

The improvement specialists taught the princess how to clean bathrooms, wash dishes, and how to change the filter in a canister vacuum. As it turned out, Princess I enjoyed making porcelain fixtures shinier.

"This is really kind of fun," she said, looking at her reflection in a clean mirror. "Is there more stuff to clean?"

The strange little barista man laughed and couldn't stop.

Next, the improvement specialists taught the Princess how to make "clean out the freezer casserole." The princess learned many things, but most important, little by little, she began to think less about herself.

PrIncess I became so fond of the pretty yellow rubber gloves that she started a fashion craze. She sold bright-colored rubber gloves to go with any and every outfit. She made millions of dollars.

Eventually, PrIncess I married a prince with a shiny red car.

She learned to make banana bread. She also started a charity organization for people who live in remote communities where there are no recycling centers.

Her complexion was always clear. Her heart was basically pure. When the princess finally left home for a new castle, her mother, the queen, turned the princess' room into a beautiful sunroom where she grew very prickly but attractive flowering cacti. The royal housekeepers returned, and everyone lived happily ever after, even the king.

Joan Gerkin

Joan Gerkin has lived in Belle Fourche since 1989. Her early years as a farm wife and mother were followed by a twenty-year career as a Fairfield Inn by Marriott hotel general manager. Now retired, she draws on her life experiences for writing inspiration.

Ghost Friends

Our joint retirement party is over, and my good friend and co-worker Bonnie and I are taking one more quick drive through the Canyon before riding off into the sunset. We have said farewell to the life we have lived at the hotel for the past twenty years. No more covering for employees who don't show up. No more making beds when there are not enough housekeepers. No more phone calls at 3:00 in the morning.

"You know, Bonnie, I really am going to miss working with you every day. I know we can now play more, but it just won't be the same not being at the hotel every day. I didn't think I would really feel this way."

"I know what you mean. There are things I will not miss, but it will be strange not getting up at 5:00 AM to get to work."

"Well, let's just enjoy our joy ride, and tomorrow we will figure out how we are still going to get together daily without my husband involved."

"Sounds like a plan."

The Canyon is beautiful, with a cover of frost on the pine trees glistening in the late afternoon sunlight. There isn't much traffic, so we can take our time on the winding road. There are a few slick spots, but my four-wheel drive jeep can handle them.

The next thing I know, we are in a spin and headed for the creek. "Hold on, Bonnie!"

I open my eyes, and instead of the creek or the canyon, I see my office desk in front of me. Did I dream that I retired? I walk up to the front desk, and Bonnie is there watching the new associate check in people. "Bonnie, why aren't you helping?" I get a funny look from her and start to ask the next person if I can help them. They act like they didn't hear me, so I ask again if I can help them. The associate has just finished with the other couple, and they move up to her computer to be checked in. Okay, I guess they don't need our help. "Let's go back to the office, Bonnie. I need to sit down. My head is killing me."

"I think I know why your head is killing you. You have a six-inch gash across the top of your head, and there is blood all over your jacket."

"What?" I look in the mirror but see nothing. Not even my own reflection. "What is going on, Bonnie? You know, you look a lot paler than normal, too."

"Let's go back up front and see if Ida can help us figure this out." There are now several of our co-workers gathered at the front desk, and they are crying and hugging each other. I wonder if someone we know died? Before I can even ask, the telephone rings, and Ida starts telling the caller that it is true. Joan and Bonnie died in a crash in the Canyon this afternoon.

"What! If we're dead, what are we doing here, Bonnie? I thought I would go to heaven when I died, not the hotel! Do you think we are ghosts now?"

Bonnie has started to check things out and is standing between Jen and Renee. They are talking to each other like she isn't there. She sticks her tongue out at Renee but gets no reaction at all.

"I think we might indeed be dead, Joan. And as a card-carrying Catholic, I think this may be our Purgatory on the way to the hereafter."

"Well, my dear Catholic friend, how do we get out of here and move on to the good life?"

"Hell if I know. I heard you must do good deeds, but I can't think of one thing good I want to do in this place anymore. So, let's just have fun with it until someone comes to get us. Follow me. I want to try something."

This is different, Bonnie leading me. She walks up to the elevator and walks right through the solid steel door without opening it first. Oh, this is going to be fun! "Let's go check out the Spa Suite." The bride and groom staying there are just getting ready to consummate their marriage. We look at each other, and without words, sit on the edge of the bed and start bouncing up and down. The couple are a little tipsy from champagne but notice right away, so we stop. They start in again, and so do we. After about a dozen "false starts," we decide to check out another room and leave them to wonder what was in the champagne.

"Let's follow this guy up to his room and have some fun," I say. We chuckle as we watch him getting ready for bed. "Not much in the manliness department, is there?"

He turns out the light to go to sleep, and Bonnie says, "Watch this." She slips into the bathroom and flushes the toilet.

Up pops the man. "Who's there? This room is occupied." He gets up to check, finds out he is alone, and heads back to bed. Bonnie gives him five minutes before she flushes the toilet again. He jumps up again and rushes to catch whoever is in his room, only to find no one there. He grumbles it must be a faulty toilet as he crawls back in bed.

We are laughing hysterically now as we head to room 115. "Remember how people always complained there was a smell in this room? Let's give them something to complain about," I suggest.

"Can ghosts still fart?" Bonnie asks.

"Only one way to find out!" I give a push, and out pops the rottenest smell I have ever had. Bonnie gives a push, and it's a double whammy. The wife nudges her husband and tells him to go to the bathroom if he's going to fart. Of course, he is denying he farted, and we leave the room laughing harder than when we went in.

I look at Bonnie, and it's as if she reads my mind. "Fire Alarm!" The sound is deafening as the guests run out of their rooms into the freezing night air. The fire department arrives, and finding nothing, allows the guests to go back to their rooms.

I say, "How about a quick swim?" We are having fun splashing around when the door opens and in walks Anthony, the night auditor. He looks at the pool in disbelief as he tries to figure out what is causing the water to splash like that on its own. We stop moving, and the water settles down. "Must be a glitch with the circulation pump," he mutters. "I'll have to leave a note for Bob." He departs, and we giggle like little schoolgirls getting caught with our hands in the cookie jar.

"Let's catch a little shut eye, Bonnie. I'm not sure if ghosts need sleep, but I need to rest this head of mine. Room 318 is empty. Let's go up there." Bonnie looks sad as we enter the room. "What's wrong, my friend?"

"Well, when I thought about spending our retirement years together, I never thought it would be as ghosts haunting the hotel we finally got out of. There is something that is just not fair about all this. We always did our best to make even the most rude and ungrateful guest feel welcome, and now we must watch them continue to whine and moan for eternity. NOT FAIR!"

"They say it's always darkest before the dawn, so let's just sit here until sunrise and see if things look better then."

The sunlight is coming in the window of my room . . . my own bedroom. My husband is still sleeping beside me, so I slip out to the kitchen and call Bonnie. "Are you okay?"

"Yes, fine. Why?"

"I had the weirdest dream last night. I'll tell you all about it when I get to work."

"But Joan, we retired yesterday. We don't ever have to go back to the hotel again. How about we meet for coffee at Patti's Place at 9:00?"

I walk back to bed and thank God I do not have to spend eternity at the hotel.

If you ever have a strange experience in a hotel, some other GM was not as lucky as I am and is just having a little fun with you.

The Impertinent Hotel Guest

Please show me the room before I stay.
  I'm quite particular in so many ways.

  I need a high floor for peace and quiet.
  At the end of the hall, with no elevator beside it.

  Clean sheets and towels daily—no, this won't do.
  What better room will you move me to?

  The parking lot lights shine a little too bright.
  Close the blackout drapes? I suppose . . . for tonight.

  Good morning—I need to be moved.
  The room last night didn't match my mood.

  I need the first floor but want a good view.
  I want close to my children, so put them there, too.

Biscuits and gravy, cereal, toast,
Scrambled eggs, bagels—you have more than most.

However, the coffee is bitter, your cups are too small.
Only apples and bananas, what's wrong with you all?

I need to be moved; my daughter got sick.
Her bed is covered in noodles—oh, ick!

These sheets look so wrinkled, please change them today.
Then this room should be adequate for the rest of my stay.

How is your daughter? We heard she was sick.
Hope she feels better soon, so she can enjoy her trip.

Food poisoning, I think from the yogurt she ate.
Can you check all your dairy for the expiration date?

Dates are all fine. What else did she eat?
There were Chinese noodles all over those sheets.

Leaving so soon? Hope you enjoyed your stay!
Please don't hurry back—but have a nice day.

Age-Appropriate Exercise

Dear Fitbit,

I've been wanting to get into an exercise routine since I retired a year ago. My Fitbit counts steps, but it must be missing out on some as I never make my daily goal. I decided to keep track of my daily routine to see where I can make improvements and get closer to that goal number.

Getting out of bed each morning—four to five sit-ups before I can finally swing my legs over the edge of the bed to get my feet on the floor. Four to five waist bends as I try to get my feet into my slippers. It must be at least one hundred steps from my bed to the bathroom and another one hundred to the kitchen to start the morning coffee. Another one hundred back to the shower, and of course the step up into the shower must count for something. Arm reaches are needed to put the shampoo and conditioner on my hair, and more waist bends as I clean and shave my legs. I think there might be a shoulder stretch in there, too, as I bring my arm up and back with each swipe of the razor. Drying off is a workout of its own, stretching in every direction to make sure all the private areas are dry. I'm beginning to feel better already!

Combing, drying, and styling my hair is a great upper body workout! Getting dressed is another combination of wriggling and stretching to get my sweater over my head and my jeans pulled up and zipped! More waist bends to get the socks and shoes on, and I'm ready to start my day.

Breakfast of bacon and eggs requires several trips to the refrigerator, bending to get the frying pan out of the drawer, and another fifty-plus steps back and forth setting the table. The Fitbit doesn't seem to be agreeing with me on my step count, but I'll keep track of it as I see it! Of course, I forgot the jelly for my husband, and he wanted a refill on his orange juice, so there were a couple more trips back and forth across the kitchen.

I'm not sure how to count my hand and arm movements as I wash the dishes and place them in the rack to dry. I think I will just add ten "active minutes." I always need more of them.

It's Tuesday, so time to start some laundry. More steps into the bedroom with waist bends and arm swings as I sort the lights from the darks. It must count as two hundred steps from the bedroom to the laundry room, especially since I'm carrying a heavy laundry basket.

At last, a few minutes to sit and rest while the clothes are washing. I can get caught up on emails and Facebook before I must put laundry into the dryer.

Back to the tugging and pulling exercise it takes to get the clothes from the washer to the dryer. Definitely "active minutes!" The second load is easier since it was already sorted, and I head back to my recliner to wait for the dryer to finish. I just sit down when my cell phone rings, and I must get up to retrieve it from the charging station in the kitchen. My husband will be home for lunch in half an hour and needs me to have something ready for him to take with him. Another trip to the refrigerator for cold cuts, lettuce and cheese, and I quickly have a nice hero sandwich made for him. A trip to the pantry, and I have potato chips, cookies, and Gatorade for him. Might as well have a sandwich myself as his looks so good. I'm sure I need to deduct some of my active minutes after I eat my sandwich and chips. But I won't.

The hardest part of laundry is folding and putting the clothes away. Takes twice as long as sorting and more steps from the dressers to the closet and back. In the bedroom, I noticed that I forgot to make the bed this morning. Steps, arm pulls, more steps, more arm pulls. A few punches to fluff the pillows, and I'm done in the bedroom!

Might as well vacuum the house while I'm at it. No active minutes here. Just push the button on the Roomba and sit for the next hour while my floor magically becomes clean!

I start to read a book as I wait for the vacuum to finish, and before I know it, the floor is clean. A couple extra hours have gone by, and it's time to start supper.

I walk outside to start heating the grill—step time again. Grab a couple of potatoes out of the pantry and pop them into the microwave. Walk to the refrigerator to take a steak out. Walk to the heated grill and put the steak on. I'm really racking up the steps now. Setting the table requires a few arm stretches again to reach the plates and glasses. Rotate the potatoes in the microwave. Go outside to turn the steak on the grill. Back inside to set the salad and the potatoes on the table. "Honey, supper is almost on." One more trip to the grill, and I'm ready to eat. Of course, once again, I've forgotten the steak sauce. More steps to the refrigerator. "Anything else, dear, before I sit down?"

Clearing the dishes from the table is as far as I'm going to get this evening. I'm exhausted. I sync my Fitbit and am dismayed that I didn't even come close to the 10,000 steps they expect me to get in every day. I may need to adjust the expectations of this overpriced pedometer to be more realistic for my retired lifestyle. Tallying my totals showed me I did indeed get enough of my own "age-appropriate exercise!" Take that, Fitbit!

If You're Not from Belle Fourche

If you're not from Belle Fourche,
you don't know the River.
You can't know the River.

The water that flows to fill Orman Dam
brings life to the crops that grow on the land.
The lifeblood to farmers and ranchers, too,
also brings beauty for me and for you.

If you're not from Belle Fourche,
you don't know the River.

If you're not from Belle Fourche,
you don't know the People.
You can't know the People.

The people so friendly who walk down the street,
take time to say "hi" to all that they meet.
The coat off their back they will gladly give,
to make sure you have the best life to live.

If you're not from Belle Fourche,
you don't know the People.

If you're not from Belle Fourche,
you don't know the Roundup.
You can't know the Roundup.

The Roundup is the grandest rodeo around.
The cowboys and rough stock all come to town.
The carnival and fireworks bring many more, too,
for a July 4th event almost too good to be true.

If you're not from Belle Fourche,
you don't know the Roundup.

If you're not from Belle Fourche,
you don't know true happiness.
You can't know true happiness.

A better life has never been lived
in any place that the good Lord doth give—

wide open spaces with time to roam,
the best in the west is where we call home.

If you're not from Belle Fourche,
you don't know true happiness.

Snapshot of her Life

A little blonde girl rides her tricycle up and down the sidewalk. When she tires of it, the backyard beckons her as a mud pie must be made. The creek that flows behind her house is low enough to get the water to mix with the soil to make the perfect pie. Her mother calls her into the house for dinner. She is not happy when she sees her muddy little girl but smiles anyway as she remembers her own youth and the pies she used to make.

A skinny teenage girl with long, straight blonde hair has replaced the little girl who made mud pies. It has not been that long ago, yet it seems like forever to her. She is in a hurry to grow up but wants to stay young. She's starting to like boys, but her daddy is still the only man who owns her heart.

Too soon, the young girl is walking down the aisle on the arm of her brother. Her daddy took part of her heart with him when he died suddenly the previous year. The handsome young man waiting at the altar for her has won over what remains of her heart. The life of a farm wife and mother await her, and she is happy.

Men knock on her door. She hears what they say but cannot make sense of it. He is dead. Is there anyone they should call? Can I hold your little girl for you?

It can't be true. I'm only 21. I'm still a child myself. How can I raise my son and daughter on my own? The tears will not stop.

The young woman is in front of the church again to say goodbye to the handsome young man—gone too soon—taking another piece of her heart with him.

The years have not always been easy for the young, widowed girl. She remarries and has two more sons. She leaves the farm and moves to the city. She goes to work as her children go to school. Day after day, she lives the life she has been given. Some days are happy, others not so much. The shine in her eyes dims as the hopelessness grows. But she does not give up.

Another man leaves her alone to raise her children on her own. This time it is not a sad thing. There is hope again for peace and happiness. There are still struggles, but with each one she overcomes; she regains a piece of her soul that she thought she had lost.

The middle-aged woman walks down the aisle escorted by her three sons with her grown daughter waiting as her maid of honor. The middle-aged man who awaits her has his son by his side. They hope to merge two families who have seen their share of heartaches into one. They know how much work it will take but are confident in their love for each other and their shared desire to once again have the dream of their youth fulfilled.

The telephone rings, and she is asked to meet the ambulance at the hospital. It is her son. Not expected to survive. Is there anyone we should call? Her family arrives to surround her with their love. Her husband of only a few months is by her side. The tears will not stop. No brain activity.

Donate his organs? Yes, he wanted that. A glimmer of light at the end of a long, dark tunnel. She will not give up on life. She has three children who still need her. Life must go on.

Days grow into weeks.

Weeks grow into months.

Months grow into years.

The sparkle returns to her eyes. The smile grows brighter as each new grandchild enters the world.

The tears have stopped. She knows they may return at any time. But for today, life is good . . . and she smiles.

The First Snowfall of the Season

The first snowfall of the season is gently falling as I sit sipping my morning cup of coffee. I am mesmerized by the sparkling crystal flakes as they cover the pine and aspen trees that dot the hillside behind my home. I could sit here all day enjoying this peaceful scene, but reality beckons. I must get dressed and go to work.

Who can really be expected to go to work and be productive during the first snowfall of the year? There should be a law that everyone gets to stay home when this annual event occurs. The date will be different depending on where you live, which may cause other work-related issues since your customers in other parts of the world are unaware that it is snowing in your backyard, but just think of the good this could create for thousands of workers across the upper regions of the world.

Twitter feeds would be abuzz with the news that it is snowing in the Black Hills of South Dakota! All businesses within a 100-mile radius are closed, and roads entering the region have been shut down. No, they are not blocked due to the snow; they are just closed because there is no one working to help you if you should have a problem. Makes sense in my world. I could pour another cup of coffee and go back to looking out at the winter wonderland and not have to worry about putting on panty hose and a suit. But alas, that law has not yet been enacted!

As I back my car out of the warm garage, I think of how it must feel to be forced into duty during the first snowfall of the season. It must get wet and dirty as trucks and cars spatter slush all over you as we cruise down the highway. The temperatures are dropping as the storm intensifies across the region. The beautiful snowflakes that have been melting on the warm highways are now starting to turn into patches of black ice. The car fishtails from side to side and then slides sideways into the snow-covered median and stops.

I sit and watch the snowflakes of the first snowfall of the season.

Life's Door

I look back over a lifetime
   of love and loss
   all gone too soon—
   the door closed on our future.
   Dreams unfulfilled—
   still memories remain
   of bright blue eyes
   and long, tender hugs!

   The pain of others
   haunts my sleep.
   I could not give up
   on the one I could not save.
   Still, I see a future—
   more love to share.
   Tiny hands
   and smiling faces!

Another door opens
and I walk through
to continue life's journey
with hope, not fear.

Angela Hastings

Angela Hastings retired to the Black Hills of South Dakota in 2010, after 25 years of service in the U.S. Army. She currently works for the South Dakota Department of Human Services as an LTSS Case Manager, assisting elderly and adult disabled individuals towards maintaining their independence. Angela enjoys the opportunity to explore our world while observing plants, animals, and people growing. She's grateful every day for the option to place words on a page towards low-cost therapy sessions, personal growth through a better understanding of herself, and a deeper connection to community.

Birthright

Vast frontier of hope.
Rolling prairie under blue.
Sparse water, with fewer trees.
Stars.
Power poles stand as crosses.

More cows than humans.
Beige faces in tangled wool.
Knee-high grass, bent by west wind.
Home.
Generations call to me.

Dashed

He appeared solid,
    strong-limbed and straight-backed,
    capable hands and quick eyes.
    Seemed to be quite the prize . . .
    and then . . . I saw him run.

Gangly, loping, awkward mess,
    betraying lack of confidence.
    Not to be trusted with my fate,
    uneven stride and clumsy gait . . .
    Why did I see him run?

Turned back in disappointment.
    Struck him from the hunt.
    No conversation to engage
    that would lead to shared old age . . .
    because I saw him run.

Marriage

It's not a race,
    where someone must lose
    for you to win.
    It's not a contest.
    There is no scrum,
    no invisible line to cross.

    It's not a tournament,
    jousting with long lances
    to knock another from their high horse.
    It's not a game,
    half sitting on the bench
    while the other sweats blood to score.

    It's a collaboration,
    building on strengths,
    focused on the future.

Red, White, and Blue Country

Red barn, trimmed with white paint,
  under a blue canopy.

  Red skin, parched by the white sun,
  wearing blue jeans.

  Red dock, dotted with white ducks,
  jutting into a blue lake.

  Red clay, after whitewater flash flood,
  broken by blue disks.

  Red ball cap, above a white jersey,
  shading blue eyes.

  Red tractor, steered by white hands,
  creating blue stubble.

Red bird, surrounded by white snow,
perched in a blue spruce.

Red stitching, on a white ball,
spirals through a clear blue sky.

Red truck, with white leather seats,
parked by a blue farmhouse.

Red comet, surrounded by white stars,
streaks through the deep blue heavens.

Redeemed

Disobedient disciple
  Striving against self
  Struggling to obey
  Whispers of the Spirit
  Lost in worldly cares
  Cacophony of doubts
  Fruitless side quests
  Fumbling in the dark
  Stumbling on stones
  Outer voice of Creation
  Speaks to my hardened heart
  Pulls me back to the path
  Tortured soul
  Turned from idols and vice
  Comforted by Grace

Sly's Kettle

Sly tried, once more, to shift the oppressive weight. His tall, lean frame was well-muscled but no match for the 1,200-pound Appaloosa pinning him to the earth. Arod, the gray mare who Sly had purchased at auction three years before, had been a steadfast companion and reliable mount. That is, until she had been spooked by a mountain lion and reared, then rolled, trapping Sly in his current posture. Sly had named her after that horse from the book that his son had liked so much. He had fallen to sleep as Sly read to him on countless nights, and the elf warrior had been his favorite character. The summer Sly had brought Arod home was the last that he had seen his boy. Where was his son now? San Diego, Chicago, New Orleans? Sly couldn't even remember. What was evident was that his son wasn't there to ride out with him, to run fence, to check cattle, or to help get this crushing weight from atop him.

There hadn't been time to consider the ramifications before shooting her in the back of her beautiful head to stop her thrashing. She had a compound cannon bone fracture, and Sly would have been crushed under Arod's weight if he had not stopped her rolling. That's usually how things worked, thought Sly. An event occurs, and we must do something in response to that event. Whether we really want to or not doesn't matter. Sly had often heard folks say that they had no choice, which was ridiculous. There is always a choice. The options may not be pretty, or even preferred, but there are always options. That's one of the lessons he had tried to teach his children. One of many they did not appreciate.

In forty years of riding over this ground, Sly had never before seen a mountain lion in this part of the ranch. Drought had brought them in from the hills, and government programs to divert water flows hadn't helped matters. Government involvement was rarely beneficial, in Sly's opinion. Always boiled down to numbers and dollars and always to the advantage of the government, never the people. Big government had no business meddling in the affairs of local entities. It was a wonder that any of the family-held ranches were still operating. Between the escalating costs and the rock-bottom beef prices, times were lean. They'd been lean before, and there was no way that Sly was going to succumb to pressures to sell out his place. Well, his mother was still living, so it was technically her place. He'd been running it for the past few decades, but her name was still on the deed.

Sly's mother was really something. In her late 60s, she still lived in and ran the main house. She planted and tended the garden each year, raised the chickens, milked the cows, made the meals, baked the bread, cleaned the main house as well as Sly's trailer, washed and ironed all the clothes, and generally covered all of the "womanly" chores. Sly wore a starched shirt, even when riding out to check cows. He glanced down at his chest and wondered if the blood-splattered, creased, crumply mess of material could be brought back to its previous state. If anyone could work that magic, it was his mother. She didn't care much for people and rarely left the ranch. She did like to paint, and the sunroom was her studio filled with both watercolor and oil masterpieces. His mother encouraged Sly to socialize, and he usually played cards each week. She stressed that it was important for one of them to be neighborly, but she didn't like it if she thought Sly was getting a little bit too neighborly with any of the local ladies.

Not that there was a wide selection of local ladies with whom to become overly neighborly. Sly tried to recall the last time he'd sat and spoken with a lady his own age. Sly had been a late bloomer with little social contact until he was in his twenties. He'd not gone to high school since he believed it to be a total waste of time. Even with his 8th grade education, he was quite bright and enjoyed reading very much. He had ideas beyond the daily grind of the weather and feed costs. It was challenging to find a lady who could relate and discuss bigger picture things with him. His wife had been quiet but highly intelligent, and he'd been drawn to her, in part, due to her imagination and capacity for elevated thinking. She had done well raising their son and daughter, and things had been okay as long as they were her focus. Once they were independent, she had wanted to do more outside the home and listened to Sly less. It had ended with him angry about her lack of obedience and her moving to Cheyenne. It was hard to find someone who was both bright and submissive, and Sly wanted both.

His daughter had inherited her mother's spark, intelligence, and wit. She had completed high school and was going into her second year of college, studying microbiology. For some reason, she was convinced that humans were going to Mars in her lifetime and wanted to be a small part of that venture. Sly had tried to talk her into more practical applications of her degree, like soil analysis, but she was set on her course. She could really make something of herself if she'd just listen to him. Every trip home, she would try to convince him to partake in one innovation or another. Their last "discussion" had been on the topic of irrigation, which Sly was convinced wouldn't be effective, so not worth the expense.

Then, there was the long-range radio set she'd given him last Christmas. Where she had gotten the money for that, he had no idea. Cell phones didn't work out on the ranch due to lack of cell coverage, and she wanted him to have the ability to communicate. They had done simply fine without radios for the past hundred years, so Sly saw no reason to use them now. He had noticed that the base unit and chargers, with handhelds seated in them, were plugged in on his mother's kitchen counter. She hadn't said anything about it, but there they were, out of the box and ready to be used. He'd walked by them as he had departed on this set of rounds. That was two days ago, maybe three. Sly was starting to lose track of time. A radio didn't seem like such a crazy idea at this particular moment.

The wind had picked up again, and it felt unseasonably cool to Sly. His left leg pinned under Arod felt damp, and he had thought it was due to sweat, but he now began to suspect it wasn't. He didn't have pain in that hip anymore. That had slowly numbed, and he couldn't feel his foot at all. Sly chuckled to himself as he thought about the fact that his competition roping and tying days were most certainly behind him. Not just because of his "old man" status, but he was certain he wouldn't be quickly exiting a mount again in this lifetime. He thought about the fact that he couldn't even exit the one he was currently on and laughed a little harder.

All that laughing made Sly realize how dry his throat was. He'd been sipping on one of his soft-sided canteens, and it was about empty. He had another, strapped somewhere to his rig. He always carried plenty of water.

Enough for him, his horse, and his dog, a large male Vizsla that Sly had brought home as a pup nine years back. He had received quite a bit of ribbing from his neighbors who all had more traditional cattle dogs, collies, or shepherds. When they had first seen Strider, with his large floppy ears, sitting on the bench seat of the pickup during a supply run to town, there had been comments that he couldn't ride in the back like a regular dog since he'd fly away in the wind. Sly had ignored their remarks since he had faith in his selection. He'd been vindicated, as usual, when Strider had developed into one of the best working dogs in the county.

Arod clearly didn't have any more need for water, and Strider had run off during the altercation with the mountain lion. That dog hadn't budged from his side when the horse had reared, and Strider had lain beside Sly for the first day. But when the mountain lion had returned that night, Sly shot at it with his Marlin 1895 and hit it. He must have just wounded the big cat, though, because Strider had taken off after it and not yet returned. Sly hadn't considered until now that his dog might be injured, and that thought made him incredibly sad. His horse was a tool, but his dog was his companion. Sly held a good dog to be worth more than most people. He would save water for when Strider returned. The dog would surely need it.

Sly was suddenly very tired. He wasn't sure how much he had slept over the time he'd been lying on the prairie. Perhaps if he rested, he could restore his strength and then shift Arod enough to extract himself. Then it would be just a short few days' trip home. As Sly started to doze off, he almost thought he heard his family name floating in the wind. He had heard what sounded a lot like *Mmmiilllllnnneerrrrrrrr* around dusk the day before, or maybe the day before that. Sly lay very still and listened. He could no longer feel the hard ground under him but seemed to be almost floating beneath the large mare. He listened as intently as he could but heard nothing beyond the blowing wind in the tall grass.

He awoke with a start. The sun was shining brightly in the mid-morning sky. The wind had abated for now. Sly squinted and saw a dust trail rising straight up into the sky, then another, and another. He could hear the faint sound of engines and vehicle horns. Sly was slightly perturbed. It appeared that half of the county had turned out to witness his predicament. Nothing to be done for it now.

"This is a fine kettle of fish," was the last thing to run though his brain as he lost consciousness. He'd never hear the end of this at next year's rodeo.

Jean Helmer

Jean Helmer is from the borderlands between the High Plains and Black Hills' Bear Lodge Forest, from classroom podiums and rural parish pulpits. This fourth-generation Dakotan serves on the South Dakota State Poetry Society Board. She was a 2024 Benetvision Writer-in-Residence at Mount St. Benedict Monastery in Erie, PA.

As You Sow, So Also . . .

You spent
  spring sowing wild oats
  summer praying for crop failure.

  Now, fall's arrival finds you
  bundling together your teenaged sheaves
  delivering them to high school's reaping rooms
  demanding wheat be harvested
  from the wild oats
  you raised.

Under Movie's Influence, 1992

Kathleen Norris reads best
  at a Poet's Society meeting held
  in an unused sheep shed
  on a rainy spring night by teens
  who illuminated her words with board-bound candles
  while, in the darkness of the surrounding corral
  ten thousand pounds of nervous and
  previously unnoticed Angus bulls
  stamped and snorted punctuation—
  a great writing prompt for next time
  when they would remember
  to check the gates

From Hammer to Old Cow

It began as an ordinary day. Ordinary, that is, for a weekend debate tournament in Sioux Falls. When I arrived at the high school at 6:30 a.m., the fifteen-passenger school van was already waiting for us. I found the keys' hiding place, then hustled into my classroom to set out lesson plans, materials, and notes for my substitute teacher. The other coach was doing likewise in her room upstairs. As usual, the kids living farthest away from school arrived first.

"Morning, Hammer!"

They greeted me using the nickname given to me a few years earlier. It both distinguished me from the other Mrs. Helmer, the school librarian, and was apropos. It referenced my extra-curricular assignments—both the wooden hammer/gavel symbol for forensics activities and the claw hammer used in building sets for school plays.

"Morning," I responded, nodding toward their file cases and the emergency blizzard kit. They grabbed the materials and headed for the van. I double-checked to make certain nothing was left behind, shut off the lights, locked the door, and followed them. An unnamed substitute would arrive at 7:45. We would be nearly to Wall by then. Cell phones were yet a thing of the future—the sub was on his/her own! I hoped my directions were specific enough that on Monday morning, I would return to classes with completed assignments in hand.

After a hands-on lesson in fitting file cases, blizzard kit, and suitcases for twelve into a small space, ten students and two coaches—along with snacks and beverages—climbed into the van. I took the first driving shift. By 6:45, we were on the road.

Four hundred miles and two pit stops later, we pulled into Sioux Falls, quickly checked into our motel rooms, and the students changed from traveling clothes to suits and dresses. Then, it was on to registration at Lincoln High School.

This was a three-state, National Forensics League tournament. We got our students signed into their events, double-checked their round and room assignments, then picked up our judging packets. While the students competed, we coaches judged the debate and individual events rounds of competitors from other schools. Competition began at 4 p.m., would end at 8:30 p.m., and would resume on Saturday morning.

After a night chaperoning our ten teens, we rousted them out for breakfast, checked out of our rooms, loaded the van, and returned to a full day of competition at Lincoln. At the 5 p.m. awards ceremony, they collected a few medals and honorable-mention certificates. We congratulated them on our way back to the van.

The students decided they wanted to eat somewhere mid-state, so after a quick stop for gas and snacks, we hit the road. It was nearing 7 p.m. If we hurried, with the Central to Mountain time change, we could be home early. "Early," for an across-the-state forensics trip, meant "shortly after midnight."

Homeward trips were always much quieter than their counterparts. We all were exhausted. It was the other coach's turn to drive.

I had begun having strong allergy issues around noon. My inhaler and antihistamines were not keeping up. My symptoms were increasing. Hopefully, rest would help, so we decided that I would swap my front seat for a student's place in the back. We chose one of the country kids to ride shotgun. They knew how to watch for the deer that were prone to darting into the roadway. I climbed into his seat in the last row.

After three hours on the road, our driver looked over her shoulder and announced a McDonald's break. I gave her a thumbs-up. Students began grabbing their coats. As soon as the van stopped, they were on their way to bathrooms and food.

While people piled out, I remained where I was. One boy stayed behind. When the van had emptied, [1] Braydon slipped into the seat beside me. By then, I was in the advanced stages of a severe allergic reaction. This was nothing new. I didn't want to panic anyone, so I had said nothing. I knew the reaction was not going to stop without an injection of adrenalin to reverse the swelling in my throat.

"Hammer?" Braydon said. He and three other debaters had been with me under similar circumstances once before. They had demanded to know the procedure for giving the shot if it ever became necessary. Their logic was sound. Epi-pens were not yet a thing, so I explained the procedure as they watched me fill the small syringe and give myself the injection.

---

1. *Name has been changed.*

"Hammer," Braydon repeated more insistently.

"Yeah?" It was almost impossible to speak around the suffocating swelling in my throat.

"You need a shot, don't you?"

I nodded but waited to move. Moving took just too much effort.

"Ham." His voice was demanding. "Do you need me to give it to you?"

I looked at his shadowy silhouette and wondered if this was a fair burden to put on someone so young.

Braydon didn't wait while I debated that issue. He grabbed my ever-present hypodermic and vial of adrenalin. He unwrapped the syringe, rapidly drew the injection, then halted. Went ramrod stiff. Time seemed to go into a freeze-frame mode. His hand held the poised hypodermic. He stared hard at my arm. His jaws tightened convulsively as fear and determined bravery fought for control.

His split-second indecision resolved, he gave a brief nod and inserted the needle with a slow-motion gentleness as though afraid of hurting me.

I wanted to say, "Don't worry about me," but by now my throat was so swollen that speech was impossible.

He eased the plunger down, withdrew the needle. The wait for results began.

He sat with me in the cold, silent van. Intermittent flashes from a nearby neon sign lighted his face. He looked like he wanted to cry, but his just-turned-seventeen senior bravery wouldn't let him.

Eventually, the swelling in my throat eased, and we joined the others inside McDonalds. Subdued by the realization of what nearly happened, we spoke to no one of the close call. Though all danger had obviously passed, we were inclined to quietness during the remaining trip home.

When we reached the school, four hours later, the students unloaded the cases into my classroom. I glanced at Friday's papers waiting to be corrected. Braydon had held back as the others left. By then, I had regained sufficient teacher composure to try to thank him.

"It was no biggie, Ham," he said, brushing me off. "Heck, I worked on a ranch last summer. It was just like giving an ole cow a shot!"

With that, he turned, sauntered to the door, and then quickly ducked out of the room. I stood, staring open-mouthed after him. Before I could recover, he poked his head back into the room.

"Hey, Ham . . ."

"A-a-a-h-h-h." My slackened jaws refused to respond.

"Later, baby!" He flashed me a lopsided grin, a goodbye salute, and disappeared. A pigeon imitation, followed by his laughter and punctuated with the slam of the main door, echoed through the midnight halls.

Echoes

I had carefully, firmly closed the door on my first career
  returning only to help a first-year coach
  arriving at the forensics tourney early.
  We configured the progression for double-entry competitors
  for varsity and junior varsity, for events' judges.
  Soon, the only remaining task was to post door signs
  identifying the locations of categories:
  Humorous Interpretation, Dramatic Interpretation,
  Duet Acting, Poetry.

  I quickly taped a sign on each door,
  quickly, that is, until I came to Room 224.
  Extemporaneous Speaking the sign proclaimed.
  Curious, I stepped inside.
  Had my old room changed?
  I entered into faint, familiar odors
  erasable markers, old books

lingering pubescent sweat.
After a nano-second pause
voices spanning three decades
began speaking extemporaneously.

I was right? You mean I really can do this stuff!
You're trying to use this to teach me something, aren't you?
Can I talk to you about a personal matter?
I got the scholarship, full ride, thanks for making me do the work.

My eyes fall on the last chair of the second row.
Skinny arms and legs still flail the air as
the boy audibly kick-shifts through gears
roars off on his invisible motorcycle
to a world beyond learning disabilities
to a place where stress cannot follow.
I trail behind him
pull the door shut
muffling the echoes of voices
speaking extemporaneously.

Dakota-Bred Guilt

It's the cursed guilt of expectations unmet

    that crawls up my spine, causes me to stare at the roads

    where last night's tracks are barely visible under morning's drifts.

    I want to crawl back into bed, spend the day

    reading, baking, snuggled in.

    But I am Dakota-bred, and my monthly breakfast

    with former classmates looms—7:00 a.m. nears;

    if I don't go, some random soul will sit in full fume,

    that I failed to predict weather, failed to cancel this gathering.

    If—when—I go, it will be me, there alone.

    I know this, but I am Dakota bred, and we keep our word.

    It's only three below—wind not much over five miles per hour,

    practically a tropical day for western South Dakota in February.

    I bundle up, take paper and pen, stay until 9:30,

    eating a solo breakfast, sipping coffee, writing the missing conversations.

Should anyone ask next month, I'll say,

"Let a little winter weather stop me? Nah!"
I am Dakota bred.
I was there waiting.
Where were you?"
Better their guilt than mine.

There's Something Fishy Going on and It Bugs Me

"Gender is either male or female,
  just the way God planned it," I huffed.
  "It's sinful to go messing with it."
  Meanwhile in the pond nearby,
  bass, triggered by primordial DNA,
  transgender to guarantee the survival
  of their species.
  In surrounding vegetation, grasshoppers who escaped
  the wet early spring and last year's pesticides
  have become self-fertile, laying thousands of eggs.
  Their next generation will return to being heterosexual.

Left mystified, I wonder—
  Is this evidence of Divine Wisdom?
  Testimony that the Creator laughs at my certitude?
  Or proof that I need to re-read Psalm 135:6?

Crossing the Line

By the fall of my eighth-grade year, failing health confined Dad to the house. Later, we would learn he'd had a series of heart attacks. Mom had taken a job in the Butte County Auditor's Office to pay the monthly bills. The Hay Creek School closed. Danny and I and five others were bused to town school. That left Dad home alone, frustrated at his loss of strength, at his inability to do the work necessary on a ranch.

I had been directed to side-track Danny on the way to the house after school, to make sure I beat him inside. That way, if tragedy had befallen Dad during the day, I would be the one to find him. Better to traumatize the just-turned-13-year-old than the 10-year-old. Sometimes there is no perfect option.

Today was typical. The 1950's era woodie station wagon that served as our bus dropped us off at the end of our lane. I pulled the mail from our mailbox, and we started toward the house, about a three-hundred-yard walk. As we neared the orchard pasture, I paused, turning to Danny. "Why don't you bring the milk cows in?"

"Sure!" Danny shoved his handful of school papers toward me. "Take these." With that, he hurried off and crawled through the fence. He was a skinny, wiry kid. His narrow leather belt gathered the extra width of the jeans around his waist. He would grow into the jeans and belt by spring, but now, the tail of the belt flapped in the wind. I could hear him calling the cows. They were as much pets as they were milk cows. I knew he'd hop onto the back of either the Black Swiss or the Guernsey and ride to the gate. Guess sometimes, cowboys actually ride cows! I chuckled at the thought and headed for the house.

When I got inside, I found Dad leaning against the living room windows. He was a study in blue. His once tanned complexion had gone to bluish-gray in recent months. His bib-overalls were noticeably baggy as was his blue chambray shirt. His elbows were braced against the window ledge. He was looking through binoculars.

He glanced over his shoulder at me. "Git yer clothes changed. Got sumthin' ya need t' do." He again raised the binoculars. He had lapsed into the southeastern Minnesota dialect of his youth. His words, rapid; his lips barely moving; he wasted no time or energy on enunciation. Something was definitely wrong.

I changed clothes in record time and returned. Dad lowered the binoculars, gave me a hard, measuring look.

"Ya need to go up there and tell those guys t' leave." He nodded to the south pasture.

"What?" I swallowed hard. I was not the Fishel kid known for confrontations.

"Ya need to take the pickup and my rifle. Go git those guys outta there. I'll load the 30-06 for ya."

Feeling my eyebrows rising, I was incredulous. Guns were for killing varmints and filling the freezer. We only touched that rifle when Dad was beside us—and he wanted me to . . .

"Keep the safety on, and keep the rifle next t' ya in the pickup. Ya gotta brace it so the barrel points down."

I frowned. Dad always insisted that rifles went in the rear window rack. That way, if one accidentally discharged, the bullet wouldn't hit anyone riding in the pickup box. I was becoming more alarmed. Blood pounded in my ears.

"Ya gotta keep it outta sight." Dad brought me back to the business at hand. "Now listen good. Ya gotta do exactly what I tell you." He put his hand on my shoulder, fixed his eyes on mine.

"Time's wastin'. When ya git t' the pasture, leave that first gate open. Go up t' where they are—but stop about 50 feet back, leave the outfit running, set the emergency brake. You got it so far?"

I nodded, repeated, "50 feet, leave the motor running."

Dad continued, "Slide outta the cab. Slip the rifle down beside you. Keep it outta sight," he repeated, this time adding, "and make damn sure ya keep the door between yerself and those guys."

Again, I nodded, but I was starting to feel dizzy.

"Tell 'em I said they're t' leave. If they want to drive past ya to the gate, tell 'em, 'leave the same way ya got here.'"

Dad's icy blue eyes locked onto mine, making sure I was paying attention. His voice slowed, and he enunciated the remainder of my directions clearly. "If they try t' argue, slide the rifle up over the window where they can see it. Then, take off the safety. If any of 'em starts to walk toward you, chamber a round and tell 'em, 'git going.' If they come any closer, pop a round into the ground in front of 'em and reload. If that doesn't do it, make the next shot count."

I froze. Dad tilted his head toward the enclosed porch indicating I was to follow him. The journey of perhaps twelve feet left him too exhausted to lift the eight-and-a-half pound Springfield 30-06 rifle from the rack above the upright piano. I took the rifle down, handed it to him. He opened the box of shells kept on the piano top, clicked five rounds into the magazine, left the chamber empty, locked the safety, and nodded toward the pickup.

"Hurry before they git up into the pines. I'll be watching. If it looks like ya got trouble, stand yer ground. Help will be on its way."

I hurried. I wasn't sure where this help was supposed to come from. It couldn't be law enforcement. Our south fence was the county line. The west fence separated South Dakota from Wyoming. By crossing either line, the intruders would be out of jurisdiction of the law. Nope. Neither the county sheriff nor state game warden could ride to the rescue. Dad was too weak to leave the house. That left me.

By the time I reached the gate into the lower pasture, the intruders were moving toward the higher hills. It had been a good year for grass, so our cattle were still up there. I hit the gas, started beeping the horn. The things in the pickup box rattled loudly as I bounced across the prairie. I wasn't concerned about sticking to any trail. I needed to get them stopped. Now.

Just at the crest of the first hill, they did. Fifty yards out, I slammed on the brakes, shifted into neutral, and set the emergency brake. Their engine stopped. Three men emerged. They looked to be in their late twenties—about my brother Chuck's age. I didn't recognize them, though.

I opened the door, slid my feet to the ground, stayed behind the door, pulled the rifle next to me, kept it hidden.

"Is there a problem?" one asked as they began walking toward me.

"What are you doing here?" My adrenalin-charged voice sounded more like Dad's than mine.

"Hunting," the driver answered.

"It's OK. We got permission," the other two chimed in, talking over one another.

"Not here, you don't."

"Yeah, we do," insisted the driver.

"Nope. Nobody hunts when we got cattle up here." I had a mission, wasn't interested in an argument.

One of the men sized me up. I saw him smirk. By now they knew I was a mere girl.

"Isn't this the Geis place?" he smiled.

I didn't budge. "Nope. Fishel's. Dad said to leave."

The driver started toward me, grinning. "We'll just head down to that gate then." He gestured to the direction I had come.

"Dad said you're to leave the same way you got here,'" I said.

The man kept walking toward me. I let him get about three steps nearer and clicked off the safety. He stutter-stepped at the audible sound. The smirk slid from his face when he realized I was holding a rifle.

"But . . ." He took another step. The sound of a bolt shoving a shell into the chamber of an aught-six is distinctive. The man stopped in mid-step. His two cronies halted as well.

For the first (and only) time ever, I pointed a gun at a human. I steadied the rifle on the edge of the opened window, exactly as Dad had ordered. I lowered the barrel to point directly at his chest. "Leave."

He froze. So did the other two. Three pairs of eyes shifted from me to the rifle, back to me. I gestured toward their pickup with the rifle's barrel. The lead man slowly raised his hands away from his sides, held them at waist-level, palms facing me. "We're going," he said. He sidled away, moved at an angle, careful not to turn his back on me.

I tracked their movements with the rifle barrel, kept it trained on them as they drove along the fence line. At a seldom used gate, they stopped, opened the gate, drove through, closed it, crossed our wheat stubble, then bounced across Brink's oat field. Still well west of Geis' eighty-acres, they exited onto the county road, sped east, rooster-tails of gravel dust-marking their flight. They weren't from Hay Creek, but word of Dad's deteriorating health was out. Probably bar buddies looking for a thrill and a kill.

Once they were truly gone, I removed the shell from the rifle's chamber, clicked it back into the magazine, flipped the safety on, and put the rifle into the window rack where it belonged. I realized I should make certain they had gotten the gate shut. They hadn't. Only the top loop was hooked. Correcting that, I noticed their tracks from earlier. They hadn't used that gate. They'd cut the fence about a hundred yards south.

We kept a few supplies in the pickup. I had enough to jerry-rig the fence back together. That chore done, I headed for the house. By then, my adrenaline rush was gone. My arms were limp. My hands shook so badly that I had trouble stretching the wire gate loop over the gatepost. I finally got it wrestled into place, drove home, parked by the door. I took the rifle and started into the house. Dad, using a wooden chair for support, was waiting on the porch.

"Give ya any trouble?" he asked.

"Said they thought they were on Geis' land. I told them they weren't, that you'd said to leave the same way they'd gotten there."

"Looked like maybe they were gonna argue with ya."

"Not after I loaded a round."

Dad gave me a quick, almost indiscernible nod. "Didn't hear a shot." He sat, gestured to take the Springfield from my still-shaking hands.

"Nah, they decided to leave." I tried to smile.

Just then, Mom arrived home. "What's going on?" Her right eyebrow raised at Dad unloading the rifle.

"Trespassers," he said. "I sent Jeanie up to run 'em out."

"You mean hunters?" Mom took the 30-06, hung it back on the wall rack.

"They were hunting all right," Dad said. "Wanted beef. It they'd a-wanted venison, they wudda stopped, asked permission. Damn poachers."

As word of Dad's failing health had spread, our incidents with poachers had increased. At night, we frequently heard shots fired from the road, watched headlights speed away. We'd lost one Hereford. Just last week, the horse we pastured for Ballenger's kids had been killed by road hunters. Gentle Blondie had been standing in the draw near the overpass. In their spotlighted hurry, they apparently mistook her white face for that of a Hereford. They didn't get beef. They killed a pet. What kind of people do that?

"They give you any trouble?" Mom's question refocused my thoughts.

"She got it handled," Dad answered.

Mom glanced at me, nodded at Dad. With that nod, I realized that, in my parents' eyes, I had crossed the line into adulthood.

Dale Kringen

Dale was born and raised in eastern South Dakota. He developed a love of reading at an early age. Science fiction and classic monster tales are his favorites. With the encouragement of two of his favorite English teachers, he discovered that writing can often be as much fun as reading. Dale enjoys his free time hiking and biking in the beautiful Black Hills of South Dakota.

Being Vegetarian in Cattle Country

It's often been said that "men are from Mars, and women are from Venus." It's also generally believed that if you happen to fall into one of those two categories and just so happen to also be vegetarian, that you must certainly be from someplace further out in the solar system. Like Alpha Centauri or someplace similar.

Nowhere is that more evident than right here in South Dakota, where cattle is king and salad is what cattle eat. Trying to explain the concept of being vegetarian isn't always easy.

To keep it simple, I usually say, "I don't eat anything with a face." Which usually brings the question, "Do you eat chicken, or what about turkey?"

At this point, I decide to bite off another piece of my tongue and simply explain that I eat neither.

Which usually brings the next question: "What about fish?" Hmmm, back to square one. Nothing with a face.

Here

Why did you bring me to this place?
    Did I do something to make you mad?
    I didn't know those were your favorite shoes.
    I didn't mean to make a mess on the rug.
    Why did you bring me here?

    I don't like this place.
    My cage is so small and awfully cold.
    There are so many others here.
    I miss my family so much.
    I don't like it here.

    Another day, another week, another month.
    Another family walks by.
    Why don't they like me?
    Am I too big? Am I too small?
    Am I too loud, or not pretty enough?

Why do they leave me here?

Who is this person that keeps looking at me?
She has a warm smile and such pretty eyes.
Should I bark out loud and wag my tail?
Should I sit nice and quiet and simply stare?
She's lifting the latch; she's opening the door!
Oh please, please, please, take me away from here!

Is this my new house? It looks so big.
It has a fenced-in yard to keep me safe.
Is that my new little boy? I hope he likes me.
I'll love him forever and protect him from harm.
This is my new family,
I think I'm going to like it here.

We've been together for a long time now, my family and me.
My little boy's grown so big, and he makes me so proud.
Together we are a family, something I thought I would never have.
But nothing lasts forever, and I'm afraid that my time has come.
But before I cross the bridge, please grant me one last wish.
Let me kiss your face, and give me one last hug.
Thank you for being here.

Isak Potz

It was closing time, and the ringing of the bells on the front door signaled the final customer of the night. Piccadilly Rose, known by her friends as "Dill," was busy sweeping the floor of the small convenience store. "I'll be right with you," she called out in her normally cheery voice. But when she looked up and saw who it was, she froze. Her blood turned to ice. Jim Hanby was a man she knew all too well. He was mostly well-liked by the people of Bonners Ferry, but there were those who knew of his dark side. He earned his living as a logger by day and a poacher by night. That was up until a few weeks ago when an anonymous tip earned him a visit from the sheriff and members of Game, Fish, and Parks.

"Take your time, Miss Rose, we have all night." He glared at her with beady brown eyes, his voice as cold as the look he gave her.

Dill dropped the broom and quickly took her place behind the register. Nervously, she smiled and asked, "What can I get for you, Mr. Hanby?" She placed her hand on the handle of the Louisville Slugger baseball bat that was hidden under the counter.

Hanby leaned in close, so close Dill could smell his foul breath coming through brown-stained teeth, and said, "What you can git for me, girl, is the hell out of my town. And that goes for the rest of your tree-huggin' hippie clan as well. But right now, a carton of Marly's will do." Dill retrieved the cigarettes from behind the counter and carefully handed them over. His tall, lanky frame, balding head, and long, narrow face gave him a ghoulish look. "Whoever it was that turned me over to the law had better hope I never find out, if you catch my drift. You have a safe trip home, darling, and thanks for the smokes."

Dill waited behind the counter until Hanby exited the building. Then she quickly locked the door. It was only then that she exhaled, not knowing how long she had been holding her breath. With Hanby finally out of the store, Dill haphazardly finished cleaning. It was beginning to get dark when she slipped out the front door. She checked the street in both directions to be sure it was safe. She walked around the corner to where she usually parked her bike and fumbled for the keys to the lock. That's when she noticed both tires had been cut clean through. No doubt it was more of Jim Hanby's handiwork.

It was late when Dill pushed her bicycle up the driveway to her home. She noticed the fresh graffiti on the sign by the side of the road. Apparently, somebody found "Rose Organics, Made Best by Nature" to be highly offensive. Dill had been living with her Grandpa Moorland and her Great Aunt Absinthe since her parents were tragically killed. She found living on the tiny farm just outside of town to be just what she needed. That is until the recent vandalism began to make things uneasy around the farm. Dill stowed her bike on the front porch and heard elevated voices coming from the kitchen. She knew something was wrong.

"Where have you been? You should have been home an hour ago!" Grandpa Moorland asked. "Your Aunt and I were worried sick!"

"I had a flat tire on my bike, actually two flat tires, and ended up having to walk it home," Dill answered. She told them about her encounter with Jim Hanby and her suspicions about him having something to do with it, but she had no proof. "I see that somebody spray painted the sign out by the road again. Do you think that Hanby had something to do with that, too?" she asked.

"Ever since Hanby was arrested, he's been looking for someone to pin the blame on, and who better than us. That man has hated us ever since we bought the farm," Moorland said. "I wish a little spray paint on a sign was all that was going on around here. I've been noticing things missing around the farm lately. And that's not all."

"What do you mean?" Dill asked.

Moorland looked at Absinthe and hesitated with his answer. "Someone's been leaving dead critters in our mailbox. It started with birds, and this morning it was a skunk."

"Moorland, something has to be done," Absinthe pleaded. "First the dead animals, and now he's harassing Dill at work. I think it's high time we get the sheriff involved."

"That old fool won't do a thing. Besides, Hanby has too many friends among the locals. It doesn't matter if we've lived here longer than most folks. We'll always be the outsiders. People don't like our kind because we're different," Moorland explained. "But I know a man who I think can help. He's from the old country, like us. Sometimes things like this are better handled in the old ways. Dill, do you know of the old man who lives at the abandoned campground, down by the creek?"

"Sure, I do," Dill replied. "Everyone knows of old man Potz. People say he's crazy, the way he talks to himself and all that stuff. But what's he got to do with Hanby and everything that's been going on?"

"Don't underestimate Potz," Aunt Absinthe added. "After all, you talk to yourself, and does that make you crazy? Potz is wise in the old ways, the forgotten ways. Tomorrow after you're done with your chores, you need to go find Potz and tell him what's been going on and that we need his help. Show him your ring, the one with the rose on it. He'll know what to do."

The previous night's conversation weighed heavily on Dill as she finished her chores. She'd deliberately saved gathering eggs for last. It wasn't that she didn't like the chickens. She just couldn't stand the smell of them. She wondered what her great aunt meant by "the old country" and "the forgotten ways." Dill carried her basket of eggs into the house and set them on the kitchen table. On it was a box of groceries and a map to Potz's place, along with a note that read, "Dill, take this box with you and give it to Potz." She changed out of her chore coat and into her grandpa's tweed jacket and wool fiddler cap. With a heavy thud, she kicked off her muddy overshoes and replaced them with her favorite pair of black Danner jump boots.

Dill picked up the box of groceries, grabbed the keys to the Jeep from the hook by the door, and headed out to the shop building next to the barn where Grandpa Moorland kept the Jeep. She put the box on the seat beside her and took her place behind the wheel. The old Wrangler coughed once, then came to life. Dill was on her way to meet the mysterious Izack Potz.

Finding Potz turned out to be more challenging than Dill had imagined. The washboard roads were stressing the springs on the old Jeep to their limits. Grandpa Moorland's map also seemed to be missing key details which caused her to double back several times. But after what seemed hours, she finally found the Tillman Road turnoff she had been looking for. Another mile led her to the turnoff to the Lone Willow Campground. The faded wooden sign hanging from a single chain confirmed her destination. She noticed a half dozen sleeping cabins arranged in a semi-circle. From the condition they were in, she could tell they hadn't been occupied for a very long time. In the middle of the semi-circle was another, larger building. A sign nailed above the door identified it as the dining hall. Only a few of the old, weathered buildings still had doors, and most of their windows had long since been broken out.

Dill parked the Jeep near one of the cabins. It was then that a small, gold-colored dog, a Corgi mix by the look of it, came running out of the nearest cabin. It barked at her a few times and quickly ran away towards the creek. Box in hand, Dill curiously followed the little dog down an overgrown path. When she neared the creek, the path opened to a large, empty area. She assumed it had been a tent site back when the campground was still open. But unlike the cabins, this one was occupied. Parked near the creek was an old camper van with its side awning extended. There was a low fire burning in the fire pit. The aroma of fresh-cooked trout floated on the air. Sitting on a stump, working on a wood carving, was an old man. She guessed him to be about the same age as her Grandpa Moorland.

Cautiously, Dill approached the camper. The miner's hat and braided gray beard told her that she had found whom she was looking for. "Excuse me, sir, are you Isak Potz?" Dill asked. "My grandfather told me where to find you. My name is . . ."

"Piccadilly Rose," Potz answered before she could finish. "We've met before. I see you already met Dog. I think he likes you. Your grandfather and I go back quite a spell. Our families knew each other in the old country. You remind me of your grandmother, but that was a long time ago."

"My Auntie A asked me to give these to you," she said as she handed him the box of groceries. Potz wasn't at all what she'd expected. Instead of a dirty, homeless loner, she was surprised to find him and his clothes clean and fresh-smelling. The silver beads braided into his beard reminded her of the pictures of the gypsies in Auntie A's old photo albums.

"Absinthe has always been a kind sort," he said. "Now, before you tell me about your problem, we should have lunch."

"How do you know we have a problem?" she asked.

"Because anytime someone shows up on my doorstep bearing gifts, it's because they have a problem," Potz said as he went to the camper and came back out with plates and utensils.

Much to Dill's surprise, Potz served up a wonderful meal consisting of fresh trout with a raspberry glaze and wild asparagus with mushrooms. As they ate, she admired the beauty of his wood carvings. Potz carved animals of all sorts. The deer, wolves, and bear were big sellers at the local craft fairs. But his favorites were the puppies and kittens that he donated to the local children's hospital. She told him of the problem they were having with Jim Hanby. She also swore that neither she nor her family had anything to do with the trouble he was in. Isak put his plate on the ground and sat in silence for a moment.

"I see," he said. "I know of Jim Hanby. A bad man he is. He used to poach around here as well until I ran him off. Your problem is that he thinks you and your family are weak. And because he thinks you're weak, he'll keep coming after you until you can't take it anymore. And then, he'll just keep coming. What is it you want old Potz to do?"

"I'm not sure. Grandpa said that you knew how to fix things like this. Whatever that means? He told me to show you this." Dill displayed the rose signet ring. "He said you'd know what to do."

"I see," he said again. "I think Dog and I need to talk this over in private."

Dill was surprised by what happened next. Isak and Dog walked down to the edge of the creek where they were clearly engaged in a very dynamic conversation. Isak was pacing back and forth and waving his arms as if in a very agitated state. Dog, on the other hand, sat calmly on a patch of grass and stared at Potz, intently listening to what the old man had to say. After a few minutes, the two seemed to come to some sort of agreement and returned to the camp site.

"Dog and I agree that you need our help. But you need to do exactly as we say." He walked over to his carvings and carefully studied them. "This one should do nicely." He picked up a large carving of a majestic stag rearing up on its hind legs and set it on the table. "Now, let me see your ring."

Dill removed her ring and handed it to Isak. He carefully examined the ring like he had handled it before. To her amazement, he gently gave the stone a slight turn and with a click, a tiny thorn-shaped blade ejected from the side of the ring. "How did you know it did that?" Dill asked.

"I know lots of things. Now, let me see your finger," he commanded, and Dill cautiously extended her hand. Potz took the ring and lanced her finger with the exposed thorn.

"Ouch! Why'd you do that?" Dill exclaimed.

"Do you believe in magic, Dill?" The tone of his voice was very serious. "Well, this is dark magic. It isn't for the likes of you. You might not understand right now, but hopefully someday, you will." Potz then placed her finger on the elegantly carved stag, leaving a deep red stain on its forehead.

"Now, lean in close and whisper the name of the one who's causing your problems."

"This is crazy!" she said. "If I do it, what's going to happen?"

"It's not for us to decide. It's up to nature. And nature will do what needs to be done. It's up to us to set it free. Now do it."

Dill leaned in close to the statue and ever so softly whispered the name. "Jim Hanby."

"Now it's done," Potz said. He picked up a heavy cloth sack and put it over the statue. "Now you need to go. You need to be home before the moon begins to rise. But on your way home, you need to take the statue deep into the woods and leave it there. Don't touch it, because if you do, the spell won't work. And when you get home, tell Moreland my debt to him is paid. Now go."

Dill followed Potz's instructions to the letter. She found a small clearing in the woods near her house and left the sculpture in the middle. The full moon was just beginning to rise as she parked the Jeep next to the garage. At supper, she told Grandpa Moorland and Aunt Absinthe about her encounter with Isak Potz. Any questions she asked of the two were quickly dismissed. But deep down inside, Dill knew that there had to be more to the story.

The next day when Dill clocked in to work at the convenience store, she couldn't help but notice Charlene Jones, the store's manager, having a very serious conversation with Jimmy Woods, the local conservation officer. "I have to admit, I've never seen anything like it. The way he was all torn up and all," she heard him say. "I guess it's true what they say about karma."

Dill held back a bit until Woods had left the store. "What was that all about?" she asked.

"I guess you hadn't heard," Charlene answered. "You know that nice Jim Hanby fellow? Well, they found his body up near Millers Pond. It appears he was out poaching deer again, and one must have gotten the better of him. Run him clean through, it did. Such a shame. He was always such a nice man."

"If you say so," Dill said softly as she gently caressed the rose on her signet ring. "If you say so."

Merlin Larson

Merlin Larson is a resident of Spearfish, SD. He has been a part of the Belle Fourche Writers for several years after taking a creative writing class through community continuing education. Since the passing of his wife, he has been inactive as a member but continues to write personal memoir.

Depth, Height, and Width

During my enlistment in the United States Navy, one of my more pleasant and relaxing memories was watching the rising sun. Following my midnight to 4 AM watch, I would climb topside and view the splendor of changing colors in the sky as the sun appeared. During those limited minutes of the dawning, my eyes and mind would concentrate on the beauty of the moment.

The horizon at sea stretches approximately 40 miles before the curvature of the earth makes any further distance impossible to see. Looking starboard, scanning to port or fore to aft, that distance doubles to perhaps 80 miles.

As I would look skyward to the stars, I would try to imagine distance in the scope of the universe that one can see with the human eye.

I would look overboard and watch the surface of the rolling waves. The eye could not see nor the mind begin to contemplate the depth of the water below. Exploration tells of the variation of the ocean's depth that extends from the shallow shores of the continents to the staggering depths of the Bartlett Trough in the Caribbean Sea that extends from the Cayman

Islands in Jamaica to a depth of 25,000 feet, or the depth of the Marianas Trench in the western Pacific over 36,000 feet, an unfathomable distance of nearly seven miles. To illustrate, placing Mount Everest on the floor of this location would leave the peak of the highest mountain on earth 7,000 feet below the ocean's surface.

Such are the words used in the scriptures that tell us that neither height or depth, nor anything else in all of creation, will be able to separate us from the love of God.

Holly Moseley

Holly Moseley lives on the beautiful plains of northwest South Dakota. She is published in several anthologies, *South Dakota Magazine*, various issues of *Pasque Petals*, and other regional publications. She serves on the board of the SD State Poetry Society and enjoys getting to know other poets through that organization.

Eulogy

When I die, choose not photos of my face.
Instead, select scenes of every place
that formed my heart and soul;
show not the result, but the whole
of who I am and how I came to be.
Where I have been and what I have done are me,
not some outer vestige lacking social graces.
No, show the memories, the moments and places
dear to my heart. Walking, exploring, abiding;
there I lived my life. There was no hiding
what I wanted, what I loved, what I needed.
In those places, my true self knew, and heeded.

Focus

An eensy, weensy spider

   invited me to play

   but I was busy working

   so I sent it on its way.

   Where it went from there

   I may never know;

   it was such a tiny thing

   that I did not see it go.

   And so it is with moments,

   they're here and then they're gone;

   and whatever I was doing,

   was it worth it, once 'twas done?

   The spider tickled my senses.

   It was red; is that unique?

   Why did I ignore it? What is it that I seek?

   What true good is busyness

   that keeps me at my tasks

instead of making a connection
when a living creature asks?
A moment lost in wonder
adds more value to my day
than all my toil and labor
can ever hope to pay.

Herbert and the Fire-Breathing Dragons

After a long winter in the caves, the dragons woke up at the first birdsong of spring. The dragons were hungry and went out to look for food. After about a week of roaming and eating whatever they could find, most of the dragons were full enough to relax a little, and the teenage dragons began their games. Like humans, their bodies were changing. All but one had started to breathe fire. Because Herbert was different, the others began to taunt him.

"Come on, Breathless, light the candles on your birthday cake," they said. Of course, there was no birthday cake. Herbert's mother and father had disappeared after a terrible forest fire a hundred years ago. Since then, rain always put out any fires before they became dangerous. People in the town at the foot of the mountain had heard rumors of dragons, but what sensible person really believed that stuff? Strange creatures were in the realm of old men and women who liked to frighten children, usually to keep them off their land. Still, no one ventured far up the mountain.

It wasn't candles that the other young dragons dared Herbert to light, but the tops of the pine trees around them. It was the young dragons' favorite game. Poor Herbert! All he could muster in response to the challenge was a cold breeze.

"Not even a spark!" snorted Teragold, the leader of the group. His sidekick, Mudrigard, chimed in, "His toenails make more sparks striking flint as he walks." Herbert tried again and only ended up frosting the branches in front of him.

"What the thunder?" said Mudrigard. No dragon he'd seen had ever failed so miserably.

Teragold studied the icy trees, then declared, "Your name isn't Herbert." He looked Herbert up and down, noting his pale brown, almost orange scales. Smoothing his own golden-brown hide, Teragold said, "No, your name is *Sher*bert, that fruity cold thing that humans like."

Mudrigard started chanting, "Sherbert, Sherbert, Sherbert!" and the other young dragons joined in. From then on, Herbert tried to avoid them, but it was not a very large mountain. One day, he ran into the other teenage dragons again. He hoped they had forgotten the last time they'd been together, but Teragold had enjoyed the attention when he came up with Herbert's nickname.

"You know why *Sherbert* can't breathe fire?" Teragold chortled. The rest of the group gave him their full attention and waited. Even Mudrigard couldn't figure it out. After drawing out the suspense a bit longer, Teragold nearly shouted, "He had bad breath!" Everyone groaned.

Herbert turned away as laughter filled the air. It was bad enough that he couldn't breathe like a normal dragon, but he wasn't going to show the other dragons how sad this made him. As he looked down the mountain, he saw the villagers looking up toward the noise of the laughter.

One person said, "Thunder this early can't be good." Most went back to their work, but two young children kept looking up the mountain. Herbert stretched a bit, trying to see them better. Their eyes got big, but then they giggled, and the littlest one waved. Herbert ducked, hoping his back looked like a tree.

The other dragons started following him around and amused themselves with new jokes about snow and cold and Herbert. Teragold often led the onslaught, trying to show Mudrigard and the others how clever he was.

"Say, did you hear the joke about the dragon that couldn't breathe fire?" he'd ask.

One of the other teenage dragons would respond, "No, are you sure he was a dragon?"

"Sure, his tail was always *a-draggin'*." When the rest of the group laughed, Teragold laughed the loudest. But Herbert's tail drooped. He tried to lift it up so he wouldn't look like the joke they all thought he was. It was a lot of work. He was getting tired.

The only break Herbert got was when the dragons got hungry again. Then they were too busy to bother with him. Each day, Herbert wandered closer to the village. The other dragons moved as little as possible after a meal. One day, Herbert was resting in a meadow, and the two children found him. He tried to blend in, but he was too big. The children ran over but stayed behind his head. Herbert almost chuckled. They were in no danger from *his* breath.

"Hello, dragon," said the youngest. "Can you talk? Are you real?"

Herbert looked at them. Though he could understand them, he wasn't sure they would be able to understand him. He didn't want to frighten the only creatures who had been kind to him. Instead, he opened and closed his eyes a couple of times.

The oldest turned to the youngest and said, "Maybe he understands. Batting your eyes twice means 'Yes.' At least, I think so." The youngest looked up at Herbert with such sweet attention that he almost cried. Instead, he opened and closed his eyes twice again. Before he could think of something else to do, a bell rang out in the town below. "We'd better get home," said the older child, and they started running. The younger child looked back at Herbert, waved, then followed her brother.

Not long after that, there was a huge blizzard. All the dragons returned to their caves. After a very long week, they emerged, hungrier and crankier than ever. After they ate, the teenage dragons decided they were tired of all the snow. The mountain was covered with it, and it was hard to get around. Even teasing Herbert wasn't as much fun.

Mudrigard said to Teragold, "We need something to do. Got any ideas?"

Teragold started to say, "What can we do with all this . . ." He turned suddenly to his sidekick. "I've got it!" Mudrigard looked confused and waited for more explanation.

"We turn the snow into our entertainment." Teragold called to the other dragons, and even Herbert listened. "Hey everybody, we're going to have a melting contest!"

Cheers broke out, and the villagers looked up, worried again. The trees were dense, hiding the dragons from sight, and the sky was clear. More quietly, Teragold said, "Tomorrow morning, meet at the top of the mountain. Everyone will take turns to see who can melt their part of the forest the fastest."

"What about the village?" Herbert asked. "Won't all the water running down the mountain cause a flood?"

Teragold nearly purred. "That's the beauty of this plan. We get rid of this pesky snow *and* we have a feast afterward."

Mudrigard added, "And with the people gone, we can roam the whole mountain and the valley!"

There was a gleam in Teragold's eyes now. "The real reason you're complaining is you know you don't stand a chance!"

He nudged Mudrigard with his elbow, who got the hint and started the chant, "Sherbert! Sherbert!"

Poor Herbert hung his head and walked away. He spent the rest of the day wishing his friends from the village would come up the mountain so he could warn them. They had stopped by a few times before the big snowstorm and were becoming more comfortable with the dragon. But the snow was still too deep.

That night, Herbert tossed and turned, trying to figure out how to distract the other dragons from their dangerous game. Daylight found him panting from a nightmare. The roof of his cave was frosted by his anxious breath. What could one small dragon do? Still, Herbert thought he should try. He showed up at the top of the mountain at dawn. "Please, don't do this!" he begged.

"Outta the way, misfit!" Mudrigard grumbled as he stomped out the lines of competition. Herbert slumped against a tall pine tree at the edge of the gathering. The smallest dragons began, but their small flames caused only a few trickles. But within an hour, bigger dragons got to work, melting waters that carved new streams. Herbert became alarmed. This was too much water, too fast.

"Stop! Stop!" Herbert ran around to each dragon. "Stop! Stop!" he cried louder.

They laughed and blew even harder. Herbert stopped running and dropped his head. That is when he saw it. His shouting had frozen some of the water. He looked back the way he had come. There were ice dams here and there. With renewed determination, Herbert flew around and around the mountain.

"What's going on?" Teragold bellowed. The dragons stopped and then noticed ice forming at their feet. Somehow, it was colder than snow, and they started dancing around. They forgot all about melting snow and blew on their feet to warm them up. Herbert circled the mountain again, making sure that no water ran down the mountain except in the streams the villagers depended on. When he was satisfied that the village and his friends were no longer in danger, he folded his wings and landed in front of Teragold.

By this time, the older dragons had noticed the extra water and shifting land. They found the gathering of teenage dragons. The Elder, Teragold's father, saw all the younger dragons looking at their leader. "My son," he said, "have you not listened to your lessons? We enjoy an easy existence because of the protection of this village."

"But they don't even believe we exist!" Teragold argued.

"And that is our protection," his father explained. Then the Elder addressed the gathering of dragons. "I fear we may need to find a new mountain. We will send explorers at dusk."

"Ahem," a small voice said. Peering around Herbert's shoulder was the little girl, her brother behind her. She walked toward the elder dragon.

"Sir, I hope you can stay. We will keep your secret." She looked up at him with the most trusting eyes, then leaned forward and whispered, "We have already. I think you know my grandmother." The Elder reared back, then peered at the little girl.

"Your eyes, yes, they look familiar. Hmm," the Elder stroked his chin with a gnarled claw. To the assembly, he said, "It is decided. We will stay." Then he turned to Theragold, "There will be no more dangerous games. It is time to teach you about living beside humans." After a long look around the gathering, he said, "Dismissed."

All the dragons left except Herbert. "What is this?" the Elder bellowed. Herbert bowed his head, sure that he would be punished for not leaving with the other dragons.

The little girl spoke again, "Sir, this is our friend. He saved our village.

The Elder studied Herbert and the children. The boy cleared his throat. "Uh, Sir, I think the village will want to have a ceremony thanking him. As we headed up the hill, our grandmother was going to see the mayor."

The Elder looked at Herbert. "Will you go into the village if they want to honor you?"

"I will," he said.

"So be it," agreed the Elder. "And if your grandmother is able, I would like to see her again."

A month later, the girl and her brother climbed the mountain again, bringing their grandmother to the Elder. Two gray heads bowed together and talked, while the children wove brightly colored ribbons along the spikes down Herbert's back. Then the humans led Herbert down the mountain.

As soon as the mayor spotted them leaving the forest, the people cheered, and a band began to play. The mayor strode forward with a large bronze badge on a chain. "Welcome, welcome, friend of our village. Thank you for controlling the flood and fire. Will you accept this medal of honor?"

Herbert nodded his head.

"Well then, your title is 'Defender of the Village.' But what is your name?"

The corners of Herbert's mouth curved up a bit, and his eyes twinkled. "You can call me Sherbert."

Irrigation/Desolation

I-70 west of the Rockies:

vines and orchards to the south,

bentonite and clay mounds to the north,

the Colorado River in between,

changing sides under the Interstate

to keep things interesting.

Did volcanoes and winds draw these lines

that I follow in pursuit of peaches?

Or was this the design of God

to teach us that not all creations

can be controlled.

People like to quip that the grass is greener

on the side you water.

And so it seems here:

the south side of the highway swells with life,

with sweetness, veriditas, and fecundity.

Across the paved ribbon, the north side simply swells.

Gray mounds rise up.

Adding water only makes them crack and erode

into rounded, wrinkled, huge humps

that stand in stark contrast

to the orchards they overlook.

Before me are lessons of mercilessness and grace.

Questions tumble within me

like the boulders in the foothills to the east:

What must break off? What will remain?

What will fly away with the wind?

What will wash off with the rain?

And will I be a stolid, barren rock

or a fertile and abundant plain?

Presence

He showed up last fall,

the day after I declared,

"We don't have pheasants here!"

to an unknown person across the state.

So there he was, challenging my assertion.

Every few days, he'd wander back into our yard

or we'd hear him in the brush,

a short "skreek-eetch,"

a cry for company, though not with us.

Then, a month of relative silence.

We figured a fox or cat or hawk

had found a good lunch;

all we found was a tail feather,

dropped who knew when.

Still, it showed no violence.

Mid-winter thaw brought shirt-sleeve warmth

and a bright red and green head above a white-ringed neck

and glossy brown body; healthy and whole.

Nearly every day after that he scavenged seeds

dropped by chickadees and sparrows.

We started leaving cracked corn

in a dish beneath the chokecherry bushes.

He claimed his spot and fended off the smaller birds

that swooped at his head,

rising up on tip-toe, stretching his neck, flapping his wings;

then he would stoop to eat his fill.

Like clockwork, just after chores,

he'd prance across the yard,

settle down in the sun-warmed soil.

One day, he started a new ritual after his breakfast:

he would rise up to full height, spread his wings,

and belt out a staggered screech far and wide

at full volume.

We became used to each other's rhythms and were content, I thought.

It might have been the first day of spring when he left,

looking for an answer to his call.

White on White

I saw the back of a rainbow,
a spatter-cloud of white
and all the colors it would show
were hidden out of sight.
I have seen the white geese flow
through blue skies, and their flight
is more amazing than we know;
their wings so soft, yet full of might.
In midwinter, I've seen snow,
a blanket refracting light
and hiding all the ground below,
holding its secrets tight.
And I have seen the lilies grow,
their pale blossoms quite a sight.
But it is night, and the full moon's glow,
that gives the most delight.

Joyce Orwick

Joyce Orwick has written feature articles and human interest columns for the *Tri-State Livestock News* and also was a column writer for the *West River Catholic.* Her first published piece was for *The Dakota Farmer* magazine. Joyce and her husband, Jim, lived on a ranch near Hoover, S.D. for 54 years raising sheep and 5 kids. They now live in Belle Fourche.

The Marrying Kind

The early summer sun was just coming up over the low hills when the battered old ranch pickup pulled away from the Ellis ranch house. The two men in the gray Ford half-ton had plenty to do that morning—drive twenty miles north to the leased pasture and check the wells and waterholes. Then make sure the bulls were doing their job. Look for any problems with the cows and their black-baldy calves. Make sure the fences were all up and the gates shut.

Lane Ellis, the rancher's son, was driving. His companion, old Tony Franklin, took a hefty pinch of chew. He'd watched Lane grow up on the Ellis place. Old Tony had watched.

Lane's dad Bob grew up on the same place. He'd worked for Lane's granddad. Old Tony was old yet even now worked sometimes as a ranch hand. He'd done all kinds of work in his life, all manual labor. Tony liked to get out of the little cow town where he had a shack, so Bob had asked him to come out and help Lane while he and Lane's mom went to visit relatives in Wyoming. Not that Tony was very active and able anymore, but he did have good ranch sense and besides, he was pretty good company.

"Your old man says you're spending a lot of time with that Peterson gal," Tony said. "You got something in mind there?"

Twenty-year-old Lane blushed. He had that fair skin which turned pink easy, and he hated that—it wasn't real manly to be blushing. He pulled his old Stetson down over his forehead and fingered his thin blond mustache.

"Well, it has crossed my mind some," he admitted. Pretty Lisa Peterson, dark-haired and buxom, crossed his mind real often.

"You been married a time or two, Tony. You gotta know something about women." Lane was eager to shift the conversation away from himself.

Tony gave the subject a little thought. "I been hitched three times, and I ain't never goin' to do it again. I'm too old for that cha-cha-cha."

"Seems like getting hitched is a lot of trouble," Lane observed.

"Getting hitched ain't so much trouble. It's the staying hitched I got trouble with," Tony responded. "That first one don't hardly count. It was one of the May-December romances, I reckon. Married in May, divorced in December. Got drafted in the army, put in two years in Korea. Right after the war, the country was torn to hell. Glad to get home—turns out nobody ever even knew I was gone.

"Two whole years of my life," Tony mourned. "Guess I wanted to catch up on what I'd missed. Met Suzy—that gal was built." Tony used both hands to draw a curvy female in the air. "Built! I couldn't wait to get hitched to all that!"

Lane grinned in appreciation of Tony's enthusiasm.

"Trouble was, she was more in love with Suzy than she was with me. Don't marry no chorus girl unless you're a movie star, and I sure ain't no Burt Reynolds." Tony rolled down the pickup window and leaned out to spit his chew into the wind. "Gotta be a good picker, kid. Looks ain't everything. Money ain't everything, either—I learned that the next time I got married."

Tony was in a talking mood. The kid needed educating, even if it came from a broken-down old fart like him! "Annie was a hell cat. She didn't start out so bad, but it all turned in a hurry." Tony took off his battered hat and scratched his head. "Didn't think I wuz making enough money for her. Then we had a kid, and it all went to hell. I wuz working on the road with Pete Gonzales. Left home early in the morning—got home just before dark, so she had plenty of time for what she wanted to do." Tony paused, leaving Lane on the hook.

"What did she want to do?"

"Well, we wuz living in a little blue trailer, second-hand, but still in good shape. Sunshine Acres—that wuz the name of the trailer court down by Hay Creek. Good enough place, I thought," Tony reflected. "Pete and I wuz headed home Monday night—close to the 4th of July, it wuz. Drove around the bend, and lo and behold, there wuz nuthin' left on that lot. No trailer house, no car, no nuthin', but a cement step where the door used to be. And my old suitcase wuz settin' on that step, and my shaving kit on top of that. That's all I had when Annie got done with me."

Lane's mouth fell open, and Tony cackled.

"Old Annie had it all figured out. Had the moving outfit all lined up to come in right after I left for work. Slick as a whistle. Pete and I prob'ly met that mover up on the highway. She had it hauled out to her folks' place on the Belle Fourche River. Cost her something to do it, too."

"How did that work out? Did she keep it? What about your kid?"

"Hell, yes, she kept it, and the boy, too. Like a damned fool, I'd put in all my savings to buy that trailer house. Thought it wuz a good investment, marrying that woman. Thought her folks had money, and I'd be set for life." Tony snorted. "The manager of that trailer court charged me for lot rent for that whole month of July, and I had to pay that, too, cuz my name wuz the only one on the lease.

"Don't ever marry for money, kid. There ain't enough money in the world worth doing that! Annie kept all my old Hank Williams records, too. They wuz the only worthwhile thing I had.

"Might as well tell you about my last wife, Delia—she wuz Pete Gonzales's sister. Didn't hurt me and Pete—we allus got along good. That marriage started out great. Delia wuz a good cook, filled me up with beans and chilies and tortillas. I gained twenty pounds that first year." He patted his belly. "I wuz working in the oil patch then, making good money, making payments on a long black Buick and a Ford pickup and a brand-new trailer house. Delia wuz like a kid in a candy store, cooking and cleaning and taking care of the baby girl when she came along."

"That baby girl would be Cecilia, I reckon." Lane knew Cecilia—a good woman who kept track of her errant father. "Sounds like it was all working good, Tony."

"Well, it wuz—til I got to drinking too much, not coming home from work 'til the bars closed. Delia had better sense than I had. I wanted to drink, and she wanted me sober. I guess I won. We got a divorce. The oil boom went bust. I lost the vehicles and the new trailer house. I had to pay child support, too.

Tony's old blue eyes clouded over. "One thing—I sure cured that woman of getting married. Don't think Delia ever looked at another man 'til the day she died—too early for that, too. Lucky for me she let me go on being Cecy's dad. Never did see much of my son. At least he wuz Annie's boy. They ended up on the West Coast. Still out there, I guess."

Tony had more to say. "If your drinking is hurting your marriage, ya gotta quit the drinking, kid. That's hard-earned advice."

They turned off the gravel road onto the approach to the big pasture Lane and his dad had leased. Lane jumped out to open the gate, even though as the driver he might have expected Tony to do it. Lane had respect for old folks and women—something his dad had always drilled into him. When he got back to the pickup, Tony wasn't done yet.

"You don't want my advice about women. I'm a three-time loser in the matin' game. I sure wuzn't always a good picker. I messed up the one great deal I had with my boozing. I took a hit from a hell cat. I got a kid somewhere I never see—bet his mother taught him to hate me. The only thing I ever did right wuz helping Delia raise Cecy. But I do know somebody I'd call a real honest-to-God expert with a hell of a track record to prove it, too."

Lane looked at Tony expectantly, wondering just who Tony had in mind.

"He's a darn good judge of women. Got himself a great one in the first place. Treats her like a queen, and she turns around and treats him like a king. That's the fellow you need to watch!"

"I sure will—if you tell me who it is I need to watch."

"Well, I don't need to pile it on with a shovel. He's somebody you bin watching all your life—it's your old man, Bob Ellis, that's who!"

Smuckering

Life in the time of Covid could be boring, especially for those of us who fell into that infamous category of *older and more vulnerable.* Luckily for me, I was able to jazz up my BLAH life for nearly a week that summer with what I called "smuckering." In case you aren't up on your condiments, Smucker is a company that makes excellent jelly. They had a memorable slogan: "With a name like Smucker's, it's got to be good," and good it is!

In 2017, I planted grape vines in our backyard, and I'd hired a man to put up supports for them, just knowing I would eventually have a bountiful harvest. We'd gotten a lot of grapes the first year, and with many things shut down, I had plenty of time on my hands. I was ready to make jelly. My vines came from SDSU via Homestead Nursery which was a wonderful provider of plants here in our town of Belle Fourche. They were Valiant and described as "hard to beat for hardiness and productivity" and "mostly for table use and jelly," which was just what I wanted.

I didn't want to be a winemaker! Been there, tried that. Another story. Wine making usually involves lifting heavy jugs, but jelly is quicker, and the jars are much smaller!

My Valiant vines were real renegades, spreading out over the grass or climbing high into the neighbor's trees. I planted another kind of grape at the same time—a small red grape with a sweet flavor. It was nowhere as flamboyant as Valiant, staying on its own trellis and out of trouble. Naturally, being so well-behaved, it has never produced many grapes.

The grapes were getting plumper and sweeter by the day. Birds were circling and flying in and out of vines. It was time for me to get to work.

I picked grapes in the cool of the early day. Then I sat on our morning-shaded deck, sorting out stems, leaves, and bugs. I rinsed the grapes well. So far, it was a joy to act like a Smucker!

I can't claim to be a great jelly maker, but I can sometimes follow directions. I didn't look at any other recipes for grape jelly for fear I would find myself running off in three or four opposing directions at once. My mantra has got to be, "Keep it simple, stupid!" So, I just simply followed the directions that came with the box of fruit pectin.

The first step in jelly making is making the juice out of the grapes. Then jelly is made from the juice. Grape juice, sugar, and pectin are all the ingredients used to make jelly, and the heaviest lifting I did was taking the pint and half-pint canning jars out of the boiling water bath. How satisfying were those sealing pops! The jelly turned out to be a beautiful deep purple with just the right sweetness and flavor!

Amazingly, my first go at making grape jelly was super successful. All week long, I had fun picking grapes and making jelly. If it had turned out tasteless or just like purple rubber, it would've *almost* been worth it. As an added bonus, along with my very purple fingers, I had jars of jelly to give friends and family truly made from scratch! All that jelly making had distracted and smoothed my Covid-ragged mind and soul. No wonder the Smuckers keep on making jelly!

Bruce Roseland

Bruce Roseland, Seneca, SD, is Poet Laureate of South Dakota, 2023-2027, BA/MA Sociology, '80, UND, Grand Forks, ND. He is a 4th generation rancher, working the same land as his great-grandfather. Roseland has written seven books of free verse poetry and won four national awards, 2007 Wrangler for *The Last Buffalo* (2006), 2009, 2019 and 2022 Will Rogers Medallions for *A Prairie Prayer* (2008), *Cowman* (2018) and *Heart of the Prairie* (2021). Roseland is President Emeritus of SD State Poetry Society and a SD Humanities Scholar.

66 miles to Reva (leaving Newell)

The winter moon makes a shadowland
on scattered snowbanks,
lighting up the flat, rolling countryside.
Crystalized snowflakes from past blizzards
give a diamond glint reflection
to all my headlights touch.
I drive north, up straightaways,
around easy bends in the road
past Castle Rock Butte
rising up in the near west, past little dips
of small creeks, past South Moreau River,
water puddled, locked frozen,
onward past Hoover, home of the 1902-built
"Oldest General Store in Western South Dakota."
I drive past small herds of mule deer

finding summer's last blades of frosted grass.

In the near distance, antelope dot open slopes,

always alert to lurking danger.

Cows graze, even in this desolate season,

where winds have blown

prairie patches clean.

Onward to the North Moreau

and across the cedar-studded Slim Butte divide,

standing like knuckles of your fist,

reaching for the stars.

At Reva, Highways 79 and 20 unite,

and north and south lanes meet east and west.

I travel a silent land.

Only far off yard lights half-hidden behind

a fold in the terrain tell me that someone

dug a toe hold and held on, pounded in fence posts,

stretched barbed wire, tended the cows,

raised their children, and passed it on to them.

Driving down Highway 79,

I hear the hum of my ride.

Looking out at the land all around me,

I'm aware of a quiet song in the night air,

a strong song.

A Prairie Prayer

Here, on this arc
  of grass, sun and sky,
  I will stay and see if I thrive.
  Others leave. They say it's too hard.
  I say hammer my spirit thin,
  spread it horizon to horizon,
  see if I break.
  Let the blizzards hit my face;
  let my skin feel the winter's freeze;
  let the heat of summer's extreme
  try to sear the flesh from my bones.
  Do I have what it takes to survive,
  or will I shatter and break?
  Hammer me thin,
  stretch me from horizon to horizon.
  I need to know the character
  that lies within.

I want to touch a little further

beyond my reach,

for the something that I seek.

Only then let my spirit be released.

Bear Butte

Looks, from a distance, like a sleeping bear
    lying alone just outside the Black Hills.
    The Butte is the result of an ancient volcano,
    a vent in the crust having not quite exploded,
    shaking off the softer rock buried beneath the plains,
    pushing up the harder rocks below,
    birthed in such intense heat its surface was brittle,
    prone to shatter, break apart, creating rock fields.
    Sharp-edged shards litter the paths to a summit,
    revealing panoramic Western views of pine-covered hills
    and mountain peaks.
    Far to the North edging the horizon, are the Slim Buttes.
    To the East, are the Breaks of the Belle Fourche River.
    To the South lie hazy plains, beginnings of the Badlands,
    grasslands, Pine Ridge.
    All four directions are represented by four
    colored cloth strips wrapped around straggly

juniper and pine trees, so too are tobacco ties offered
by vision seekers, those searching for clarity
after four-day prayer ceremonies.

The remains of trees burnt
to their stumps by devastating reoccurring fires
are scattered across the slopes to the very top.
At this narrow ridge of summit
mule deer graze and rest next to boulders unafraid,
protected by the forest service.
Far below, cattle drink from stock dams,
the water provided by cloudbursts and melting snow
running down this steep-sided, rocky butte
the natives call sacred,
sublime, Holy.

I feel the pull of another year

Light drizzle is coming down,
    puffing on an easy wind,
    just enough to let you know it's wet.
    A thermometer tacked on an outbuilding wall
    says 50 degrees, the start of cooling toward winter.
    Fall run of calves has begun
    at the local livestock auctions,
    meaning money in the pocket,
    rewards reaped from the hard, cold, wet spring
    we all went through.
    Possible calf losses loomed each day,
    the muck was deep and the odds didn't
    look very good.
    Still, months later, on a morning like this,
    when the damp cool is in the air,
    my thoughts drift forward,
    just like the seasons changing,

turning toward a new year.
I'll be drawn again to check on the life
being born in the lots,
making sure nothing has gone wrong.
I'll eagerly wait for a calf's first gasping breath,
and those wobbly first steps on legs newly outstretched,
instinctively nuzzling toward
the warmth of a waiting mom.
I see myself there, part of this scene,
wet wind on my face, hunkered in my work clothes,
the scent of earth and sky, cow and calf,
in the air.

Remember me

A mile east of my homestead
  is a shallow valley at the headwater
  of Medicine Creek, which runs northeast
  to southwest 75 miles as a bird flies,
  eventually emptying into the Missouri.
  On the eastern slope of the creek,
  a spot of different-colored soil marks
  what's left of my great-grandparents' soddy,
  abandoned after catching fire,
  nearly killing Great-Grandmother Elizabeth.
  On the west bank of the slip of a creek bed
  is the faint remains of a dirt dugout,
  temporary shelter of an unknown
  where I found an arrowhead among the sod.
  A quarter mile west on the flat of a hill,
  lies the grave of children,
  brother & sister,

who died in the early 1880's
from diphtheria, buried here
before nearby town cemeteries
were established.
Their grave is a small 4-foot by 4-foot plot
lined with field rocks.
A dip in the earth 75 feet to the southwest
marks where their parents' soddy stood.
Here frequently the wind blows,
and the grass still waves in the breeze.
The geese in the fall fly south--
soon after, snow covers the plains.
The geese in the spring fly north—
snowmelt fills the buffalo-made wallows.
I am now one of the few who knows
what these things mean.
When I am gone, who will remember?

What was lost is found

The Blizzard of April 13, 1986, was nasty,

a wet, cold blow lasting three days.

Temperature hung at 18 degrees,

wind up to 90mph created a screeching white-out.

The storm sprung suddenly in the night.

When the first flake hit,

I had 100 newly born calves on the ground,

in far, open lots, with nothing

but an old hay rack for shelter.

By morning, I knew that yesterday was addition

for my herd and that going forward would be subtraction.

I had no cab on my small tractor, no way

of bringing them closer to better shelter.

I could only stare out into the madness

of wind and white, seeing at most 100 feet in daylight,

not daring to venture out to check the pairs,

afraid I would only startle the cattle,

causing them to drift further away,

piling them into and over snow-covered fences.

Later I heard of neighbors who had managed

to bring their newborns closer to tree breaks or buildings

only to have them buried under deep drifts,

smothered by snow and ice.

When the blizzard died down as light broke the third day,

the cattle yards looked like battle fields,

with ice encrusted lumps of calves,

having been blinded by the storm, fallen,

almost randomly placed across the lots.

Mother cows walked from silent, still calf

to silent, still calf, trying to find what they had lost.

The surviving, standing calves, their hair coats

matted, hanging thick with ice and snow,

cried for mothers, some getting paired up.

I checked each downed calf lying stiff on their sides,

half buried by drifts. Some blinked

when I threw snow into blank, staring eyes,

the only way I could tell they were yet alive.

These living I carried back into a closed shed

to thaw out the best they could.

When the calves stood up on their own,

I carried them back, pushing them toward the herd.

Frantic cows came rushing up, bellowing, seeking their lost.

Sometimes three cows would fight over a single calf,

each trying to nudge it from the other.
Not one calf was left unclaimed.
Out of 100, I lost 40 calves.

Several days after the storm let up,
I was out giving antibiotics to calves with frozen feet, ears, tails.
Far out in the prairie, past my snow-covered fence,
I spied a dark form moving nearer, crawling. A coyote?
No, a calf, that had lain down in prairie grass
and had become covered by a shallow snow drift,
not smothered or frozen, but sheltered.
The calf, hearing cows' bellowing, had decided to rise up,
crawl out of its tomb of snow and live.
I walked out in knee deep snow
and brought the calf back to the herd.
Like magic, his mother appeared,
and the calf went straight to nursing.
All around the snow was diamond bright blinding white,
and the sky was deepest blue.

Publishing Credits

Margaret Bolte, "A Compassionate and Caring Community," in *Belle Fourche Beacon*, December 22, 2021, p. A5.

Margaret Bolte, "Overheard Conversations," in Scribes Valley's *Anthology 20*, Knoxville, Tennessee, 2023, pp. 49-53.

Angela Hastings, "Marriage," in *Pasque Petals*, fall, South Dakota State Poetry Society, 2023.

Angela Hastings, "Red, White, and Blue Country," in *Pasque Petals*, spring, South Dakota State Poetry Society, 2023.

Jean Helmer, "Dakota-Bred Guilt," in *The Green Elephant, 2023 Scurfpea Anthology*, Scurfpea Publishing, Sioux Falls, SD, 2023.

Jean Helmer, "Echoes," in *Pasque Petals*, vol. 98.2, fall, South Dakota State Poetry Society, 2024, p. 94.

Jean Helmer, "There's Something Fishy Going One and It Bugs Me," in *The Green Elephant, 2023 Scurfpea Anthology*, Scurfpea Publishing, Sioux Falls, SD, 2023.

Jean Helmer, "Under Movie's Influence, 1992," in *Pasque Petals*, fall, South Dakota State Poetry Society, 2023, p. 96.

Bruce Roseland, "66 miles to Reva," in *The Green Elephant, 2023 Scurfpea Anthology*, Scurfpea Publishing, Sioux Falls, SD, 2023, p. 64.

Bruce Roseland, "A Prairie Prayer," in *The Cattle Business Weekly*, Phillips, South Dakota, May, 2022. Also, in *South Dakota in Poems*, edited by Christine Stewart-Nunez, South Dakota State Poetry Society, 2020, p. 85. As well as, in *A Prairie Prayer* (Gold Medal Winner of the Will Rogers Medallion in Western Poetry), North Dakota Institute for Regional Studies, North Dakota State University, Fargo, North Dakota, 2008, p. 1.

Bruce Roseland, "Bear Butte," in *Pasque Petals*, spring, South Dakota State Poetry Society, 2021, p. 21.

Bruce Roseland, "I feel the pull of another year," in *Pasque Petals*, fall, South Dakota State Poetry Society, 2020, p. 56.

Also, in *The Cattle Business Weekly*, Phillips, South Dakota, October, 2019.

Bruce Roseland, "Remember Me," in *Pasque Petals*, spring, South Dakota State Poetry Society, 2022, p. 45.

Bruce Roseland, "What was lost is found," in *The Green Elephant, 2023 Scurfpea Anthology*, Scurfpea Publishing, Sioux Falls, SD, 2023, pp. 62-3.

Acknowledgements

Life's Landscapes is the culmination of work produced by writers in the Belle Fourche, South Dakota region. That a group of people with stories to share should come together for this length of time is significant. That the group has continually encouraged the talents and missions of its members is even more noteworthy.

Life's Landscapes is the product of several years of writing and editing together. It follows the first Belle Fourche Writers anthology, *Roots Grow Deep and Strong*, published in 2012. *Life's Landscapes* represents the efforts of a dedicated and talented team.

Thanks go out to our anthology committee, many of whom are original members of the group: Eric Beeman, Jean Helmer, Joan Gerkin, Margie Bolte, Lynda Edwards, Angela Hastings, Meg English, and Kathy Bjornestad. Special thanks to Kathy Bjornestad of Beartown Press for her professional publishing expertise, to Angela Hastings for the interior artwork, to Meg English for the cover design, and to John English for help with formatting the cover art.